The Old Boys

Also by Kirk Winkler

Eva Rae's Song
The Intruders

The Old Boys

A "Marshals of the West" Novel

Kirk Winkler

*To my parents,
for their love and faith*

Chapter 1

THE TRAIN RACED NORTH PAST CASTLE ROCK and into the valley of the South Platte. Thick black smoke and cinders billowed from the stack and dissipated in the crystalline air as the fireman shoveled coal into the firebox; the great drivers turned the wheels so smoothly over the steel rails that the huge black engine moved through the gentle curves at sixty miles per hour without causing so much as a discomforting jolt to the passengers in the sleepers and smoking cars.

The engineer, peering out the open right-hand window, let the sweet winds of late September blow into his face. It was a perfect day. The browning plains fell away eastward to the edge of the world; on the other side of the tracks, the tree-covered ramparts of the front range lifted ponderosa and aspen thickets and grassy meadows toward the sky; beyond them, the granite upthrusts of the heart of the Rockies reached for the sun, the barren slopes above timberline already buried in a white cap of snow.

The engineer smiled. He would see those mountains on tomorrow morning's return run.

***

The gentleman in the smoke car had an excellent view of the mountains already, but he wasn't interested in them at all.

He leaned back in the leather-covered seat, pulled his pocketwatch from his vest for the twentieth time in the last two hours, and flipped open the silver case with thick, well-manicured fingers. Scarcely five minutes had passed since last he'd looked. He snapped the case shut with some irritation and smoothed his well-tailored vest, pulling it down a little to help cover his more than ample girth. The good black cigar clenched between his teeth had gone out; he chewed absently on the stub but didn't relight it.

Another passenger walking back from the dining car grinned and nodded, recognizing the important gentleman, who merely scowled and looked quickly away to cut short any possibility of idle and unwelcome conversation.

Impatiently, he folded his thick fingers over his vest, restraining the urge to look at the watch again. He wished idly that he had hired a private car for this trip, but an extravagance of that sort was out of the question. Had the trip been longer, he would have done it, but he was no wastrel; the additional cost for so short a journey would have been altogether too high and would have caused more comment and speculation than he could afford.

He reached into his vest pocket again from habit, but caught himself and left the watch where it was.

The Platte came into view off to the west. The river was low this late in the year; only a little ribbon of muddy water trickled among the sandbars.

The engineer blew the shrill steam whistle; a flock of

wading birds took off from the river's edge in a cloud, then wheeled and returned to their feeding as the train roared past.

The gentleman watched the birds without interest. Unable to wait any longer, he checked his watch again and sighed.

So much longer to wait.

He wished he had the power to make time go more quickly. So he could finish with this unpleasant but altogether necessary little act of murder and get on with the pressing business it had so inconveniently interrupted.

Chapter 2

TOM ALVAREZ'S BAD RIGHT LEG HURT LIKE SIN, which didn't make any sense at all.

The old injury often pained him in cold or wet weather or, for reasons he didn't quite understand, when he was in danger. But this was a perfect early autumn day, with the sun shining a warm and benevolent yellow on all the world. The central Colorado plainsland rushing by the daycoach window was ripe with heavy-headed September grass and sunflowers, and fat Herefords scattered across the lush countryside looked up from their casual browsing only long enough for the train to pass. Even along the western horizon, where the purple mountains rose up out of the plains like some great wall marking the end of the earth, no storm clouds gathered to break the blue vault of sky.

And still his leg hurt, deep inside the knee and thigh.

Alvarez lifted himself up and adjusted the blue plush pillow he'd been sitting on for a hundred miles. Perhaps the leg ached only because of the constant jostling of the train, or perhaps it was nothing more than fatigue.

If that was the reason, he'd be able to rest soon enough. The train was barely an hour away from Denver's Union Station, and the old Drovers Hotel wasn't far from there. There'd be plenty of time to get some shut-eye before he had to meet the boys.

The boys.

Alvarez sighed and lowered his battered old black hat over the hawk nose, then closed his steel-gray eyes and tried to visualize these old men he expected to see after such a long time. Bill Tilghman from Oklahoma would be there, tall and serious and straight, the lawman's lawman. Then there'd be Wyatt Earp from California, rat-faced and paunchy with age and still more interested in lying about the OK Corral gunfight than in telling the truth about it. Bat Masterson, round and jolly, wrote the sporting news for New York newspapers now, or so it was said. And there would be others—dozens of them. Ben Comstock from El Paso, the talker with a mean streak that bore careful watching. Arnold Toothacker, the alcoholic from Pueblo, would be there because the convention was practically in his own back yard and because the drinks would be plentiful.

Some would be missing, of course. Pat Garrett was dead, shot down two years before, and a few others had died along the way—some in the line of duty and some from old age. But most of the old-timers who were left were coming, nearly a hundred men with nothing better to do than waste three days in Denver swapping lies with one another about their old outlaw-hunting days. There would be newspaper reporters and photographers and the fellows from the pulp magazines back East, all eager to dredge up the old yarns to retell to the reading public. And the old boys would, likely as not, be only too glad to oblige.

Alvarez still wondered exactly why he'd decided to come. He told himself it certainly wasn't a burning desire to see most of his old comrades.

Maybe his wife was right. Maybe he just wanted to talk about the old times, too.

The thought left a bad taste in his mouth.

Back in his active days, Alvarez had considered it a weakness to talk about the job. Manhunting was hard and cruel work, taken up for a hundred reasons, including the money. To do the job right took a lot out of a man, make him do things ordinary men would fear him for, so it was always easiest and best for the lawman to keep his own counsel, to keep what he thought about the job inside, bottled up. The ones who bragged about manhunting, who were in it for the glory, usually wound up dead. To be a successful lawman—or at least a surviving one—was to be a loner. Alvarez had been a loner in the old days, and a loner he'd stayed. Yet here he was, riding a daycoach into Denver for a convention of old-time peace officers the backers had billed as the rowdiest convocation to hit the city in years.

Alvarez prayed the backers were wrong. He hated public spectacles. In fact, he hated the public, period. Always had, he supposed. He'd spent thirty years as a federal marshal upholding laws he despised more often than not, serving blind justice because it was his sworn obligation to do so and because the public paid him to do it. They'd never paid well, God knew, but they *had* paid, so he'd done his best to do his job. He'd kept the public safe so they and their weak-chinned offspring could prosper and multiply until they crawled all over the finest land God had ever put on earth, despoiling it, turning it to the plow, filling up the old buffalo range with their stupid Herefords, building ramshackle towns and railroads where Comanches and Arapahoes had once spilled one another's blood.

So why was he going to the convention?

Perhaps because he knew in his bones this was the last time he would see these men.

Men who understood. Who were here when the land was young and green and without law and altogether better than it was now. Men who needed to brag a little and share their exploits now that their own best days were behind them.

Men like himself.

Alvarez sighed again and allowed himself to doze a little just to see if it would ease the ache in his leg. The monotonous clacking of steel wheels on iron road soothed him. He drifted, and slept.

The conductor shook him wake. "Denver Union Station just ahead, sir," the conductor said almost apologetically, then moved down the line to inform the other passengers.

Alvarez sat ups straight and rubbed his knuckles across his eyes and adjusted the pillow one last time. The city was flying past his window. Row on row of frame bungalows on the outskirts gave way to the sedate two-story brick dwellings nearer the center of town. The gold dome of the state capitol rose out of the lowlands along the meandering South Platte, and the brown brick jumble of downtown Denver came into view.

The train slowed as it entered the clutter and confusion of the railroad yards. Sweating laborers mending track or cleaning Pullman cars looked up as the train passed. The engine braked and the cars banged together and rolled slowly to a stop with a final hiss of steam and the metallic grinding of locked wheels.

"Denver Union Station! This car stops here!" the conductor sang out from the front of the daycoach.

Alvarez rose and put his weight carefully on the right leg until he was sure it would hold him, straightened his rumpled black wool suit as well as he could, and retrieved his worn valise from under the seat. He waited until the other passengers got off, then hobbled down the aisle. It's only the gentlemanly thing to do, he told himself, but he knew that was a lie: he didn't want the women and children and younger men on the train to see him limping like an old man.

The conductor tipped his hat as Alvarez clumped down the steel stairs and stepped off onto the two-step box a porter had put in place.

"Have a good stay in Denver, sir!" the conductor said cheerily.

Alvarez glared at him in a way that had once brought terror to the hearts of grown men, but the conductor didn't seem to notice the look, or to care.

"Watch your step now!" he said.

Alvarez gritted his teeth against the throbbing in his leg and hobbled across the broad plank platform and into the station. People were everywhere—tired-looking women and dirty-faced children, farmers and ranchers and bankers and clerks, even a few Indians in tattered ceremonial dress, obviously there solely for the benefit of the tourists coming into the city. Alvarez made his way through the throng and passed beneath the stone arches into the streets of Denver.

The day was warm and the air crisp and dry from the altitude, yet still his leg hurt.

"Sitting too damn long," he said aloud, deciding to walk to his hotel as to spite the old injury.

Just moving felt good, as it always had. The streets were alive with the crush of commerce. Horses and hansom cabs and delivery wagons and schoolboys and businessmen and sunburnt ranch hands were everywhere. A horseless carriage chugged out of one alley and turned up another, leaving a cloud of stinking blue smoke in its wake. The air smelled of horse dung and coal dust and the assorted grime of a city, and Alvarez decided that on balance the natural smell of the horses was the best of the lot.

The Drovers was a magnificent old edifice of red brick and wrought iron, a showplace set across from a little park where old men played checkers in the September sun. Alvarez nodded to the doorman and stepped into a cavernous lobby reeking of stale cigar smoke and unwashed spittoons and many manure-covered boots. He found these familiar, masculine odors altogether to his liking. A few sparse electric lights did little to dispel the darkness of the paneled walls, green felt carpeting, and heavy red velvet draperies, but after the brilliance of the sun-drenched afternoon, this too was comforting.

Alvarez registered, then carried his valise up to his room.

The upper floors were even darker than the lobby. Each floor had a bathroom with cold running water—guests could have hot water hauled up from the kitchen, the man at the desk had said—and the rooms were ample if not luxurious.

In Alvarez's room, the one large window overlooking Larimer Street was open, the breeze rustling the curtains. He tested the bed. The mattress was firm, without lumps, and when he pulled back the cover, he found the sheets crisp and clean. He opened his valise and emptied the contents into the bureau: a pair of trousers, two clean shirts and some spare paper collars, two pairs of long johns, stockings and some garters, a razor and soap and a strop, and a well-oiled Smith and Wesson revolver. He hefted the ancient gun, feeling the balance in his hand. It was an awkward weapon, really, one that had never caught on the way the more elegant and simple Colt had, but Alvarez was partial to it for reasons he could no longer quite specify. He laid it on the long johns and shut the drawer, then hung up his black coat, pulled the suspenders off his shoulders, and stretched out crosswise on the bed to accommodate his height.

He went to sleep again almost instantly, but even in his sleep the leg nagged at him.

He awakened instantly at the sound of knocking on the door, but it took him a few moments to get his bearings; the first clear thought he had was that the old instincts, the split-second decision-making abilities that had saved his life more than once, were getting rusty from lack of use.

"Who is it?" he barked, trying without much success to sound irritated instead of sleepy.

Whoever it was knocked again.

Alvarez rose and thought about the Smith and Wesson in the drawer and then purposely ignored it. This was the second decade of the twentieth century in downtown Denver, after all; he hadn't needed that old gun in years. He went to the door and pulled it open.

A tall man with graying sandy hair and well-muscled arms folded across a barrel chest stood in the center of the hallway where the light from the gas jet fell on him, lending his face a shadowy air of mystery, making it impossible for Alvarez to see whether mirth or malice lingered there. His eyes were hooded, with lips that drooped; Alvarez remembered the eyes and the man at once.

"What the hell do you want?" he snorted, but the gruff tone couldn't quite mask the pleasure he felt.

A crooked grin worked its way across the lower half of the caller's face. "By damn, Thomas, you ain't changed a tic in fifteen years!" The voice was high-pitched and Texas-twanged, exactly as Alvarez remembered it.

Alvarez nodded. "You neither, Ben."

"I wake you up?"

"Yes."

"You don't look none too happy about it."

"I'm not."

"Old fellas like you need plenty of rest, huh?"

"Old fellas like you and me."

The grin spread all the way across Ben Comstock's face, and the hooded eyes opened a little. "As I recall, I'm some younger'n you. I won't be sixty for two months yet. You've already crossed that great divide, ain't you?"

Alvarez didn't say anything.

"Thought maybe I'd buy you a drink," Comstock said. "'Course I realize old farts like you can't hold your liquor like us young bucks."

"You talk too much, Comstock," Alvarez said, and the warm laugh came bubbling out of him in spite of his best efforts to hold it back. He hitched up his suspenders and followed Comstock downstairs.

"You still ain't a big drinker, are you?" Comstock asked

seriously after the bartender had delivered his second neat whiskey. He propped his chair against the dark saloon wallpaper and tossed down the drink.

Alvarez played with his own shot glass before taking a sip. "No, I'm not."

"Your bum leg getting worse?"

"It troubles me some."

"I reckon I wouldn't drink neither with a bum leg."

Alvarez shrugged. The leg had nothing to do with why he'd never been a drinker, but if Ben Comstock was too stupid to understand instinctively that a good lawman shouldn't drink hard liquor, then that was his problem.

"Must be a bother to have a gimp leg like that," Comstock said, pressing the point.

"Must be a bother to talk as much as you do. Keeps you from having too many friends," Alvarez growled. Pushing too hard had always been one of Comstock's biggest failings. Alvarez took another sip of his own whiskey in self-defense. He had to admit it was good liquor, probably a fine Kentucky sour mash. The Drovers would have put in a supply of first-rate liquor for the convention on the sensible theory that the out-of-towners would want to keep their whistles wet and, when they returned home, could be depended on to spread the word that this was a quality hotel. "You always were a hell of a talker, Ben," Alvarez added, just to make sure he got the point across.

Comstock's hooded eyes brightened a little, and a half-grin played across his face. "Maybe so." He nodded in the direction of a man entering through the door leading into the lobby. "If you want the silent type, there's Bill Tilghman."

It was Tilghman, all right, tall and ramrod straight

except for the beginnings of a little potbelly protruding from under his vest. His high-crowned white hat and walrus mustache couldn't be mistaken. Alvarez waved and Tilghman waved back.

"He's still marshalin' in Oklahoma, if you can believe that," Comstock said. "He's maybe a little younger'n us, but he's damn sure no pup, and he's still at it. Were I him, I'd put my feet up and let some other fellas do the lawin'. That's rough country down there. Not as rough as El Paso when I was marshalin', but plenty rough just the same."

"Oklahoma's hard country, all right," Alvarez agreed. In all his years in the service, he'd dreaded having to go manhunting down in the Nations the most.

"Not as rough as El Paso, though," Comstock repeated. "You got to admit that."

"Bullshit," Alvarez grunted, and he tossed back the whiskey.

Comstock chuckled. "You ain't going to get my goat that easy. Not anymore."

"Too bad." Alvarez was in fact a little disappointed; pushing and prodding Comstock to the brink of explosion had been daring and dangerous sport in the old days.

"You see the paper?" Comstock asked with another little chuckle of pleasure. "There's a story in it about us. The convention, I mean."

Alvarez shook his head. "I haven't had time to read the papers." Reading had been one of his great passions in the old days, sometimes devouring two newspapers a day when he could get his hands on them and always *Harper's Weekly Magazine* and the *Police Gazette*, but since he'd laid down his badge and gone home to putter around his wife's flower garden, his interest in the world had diminished to a point where he might go a month at a time without reading anything. His wife still took the Wichita paper, but mostly to have something to wrap the garbage in, which seemed to be just fine with her. He realized suddenly how very much he missed it.

Comstock waved over a waiter and asked for a copy of the *Rocky Mountain News.*

"Read it for yourself, Thomas," he said.

Alvarez scanned the sheet and found the headline, but that was the best he was going to be able to do. "Dammit, Ben, I can't read this thing without my glasses."

"Well, hand it back and I'll read it to you." Comstock snapped the paper between his hands with a flourish, squinted at the print, and began reading. "Says here…

"Fourscore old-time peace officers are set to gather in our city, beginning this evening, to relive their deeds of courage in days gone by. The lawmen, most of whom are retired from active service, come from all over the old frontier. All served the cause of peace in the formative years of our western settlements, having taken up badge and gun in the last three decades of the last century. They were sheriffs, constables, deputies working with the Pinkerton Detective Agency, or members of the federal marshal service."

He turned the page and juggled with the paper for better light.

"Some famous names are to be found among the attendees, including such luminaries of old-time justice as Wyatt Earp of the OK Corral fight, John Poe of New

Mexico who helped bring Billy the Kid to his rightful end, Colorado's own Arnold Toothacker, and others whose exploits are perhaps not as well known but nevertheless as deserving of our praise. These former lawmen will convene at the historic Drover's Hotel, where the hostelry's accomplished staff will provide them with room and several sumptuous banquets."

He chuckled and took a sip of whiskey. "And wait'll you get a load of this!" He found his place and began reading again.

"Special guest of honor for tonight's event will be none other than the great hero of the old West and frequent visitor to Denver, Colonel William Frederick 'Buffalo Bill' Cody. The famous hunter, Indian fighter, and showman is currently residing in our fair city while he conducts business. Several additional events are scheduled for Friday and Saturday."

Comstock laid the paper down. "What do you make of that one, pard?"

Alvarez sniffed and shook his head disapprovingly. "That sonofabitch is the biggest windbag west of Kansas City."

"Worse than me?"

Alvarez didn't even try to hold back the laugh. "Worse than you, Ben. Actually, he may be the biggest windbag in the world, and Lord knows he's had plenty of chances to prove it."

"Well, he was in town and finagled his way into an invite."

Alvarez signaled the waiter. "In that case, I will have me another drink of this fine Kentucky whiskey."

The two of them sat at the bar for what was left of the afternoon, Tom Alvarez drinking carefully and Ben Comstock tossing the shooters down while the place filled up with fleshy, gray-haired men. The average age was somewhere above fifty-five, old for men in their profession. Alvarez remembered most of them in spite of the passage of years. Some had been Pinkertons as far back as the seventies, when the James Gang was on the loose, and had stayed on to bring the Daltons and the Hole-in-the-Wall bunch to justice. Others, come West with the Black Hills gold-seekers, had been through the rough-and-tumble days in Deadwood and Cheyenne. Some had done a little scouting for the army during the last years of the Indian troubles. Others, like Tom Alvarez himself, had first pinned on their badges in the hell-raising days of the Texas-to-Kansas cattle drives, when the longhorns were coming north by the tens of thousands, the spiderwebs of railroad tracks were going west, and the last of the great buffalo herds were falling to the guns of the hide hunters. In those days, a lawman might have to bust heads on drunken cowboys one day and hunt down man-killing Comancheros the next. And now here they were, all of a single mold: old men with untrimmed mustaches on puffy, windburnt faces, fat bellies rolling over steer-hide belts, rumpled white shirts and cellulose collars wilted, and old-fashioned wool suits worn thin in the seat. Although Wyatt Earp, who was already holding court at a large table near the door, and a few others had some money and wore it well, the majority had never made decent wages, had been notoriously bad businessmen when given the chance, and so had long since settled into genteel poverty. For the most part, they looked to be a sorry and sour lot, men whose day was past.

Except, it seemed, for Ben Comstock.

Alvarez decided that perhaps he'd misjudged Comstock all these years: the man was a convivial companion, given to easy laughter and self-deprecating humor—not the sort of tense, angry, violent man that he remembered. But of course, Ben Comstock had been a working lawman in those days, as had Alvarez, and the work weighed a man down, changing him subtly, making him somehow different from what he might otherwise have been. Sometimes those changes stayed with a man even when the lawing was done, but perhaps Comstock had been lucky enough to find a way to get the job out of his system in a way Alvarez had not.

"Look there!" Comstock said as he dug into his pocket for greenbacks to pay for the last round of drinks. He pointed toward a corner along the far wall and a thin little man Alvarez hadn't noticed until now. The man sat alone, hunched over a half-empty bottle of rye. He looked eighty. "I do believe that's Colorado's own Arnold Toothacker."

Alvarez sniffed. He remembered, fleetingly, a young and wiry Arnold Toothacker riding through the night to surprise a nest of Comancheros. Or Toothacker, fearless in the face of a drunken ax-wielding miner twice his size, disarming the man and wrestling him single-handedly to a makeshift jail. But mostly he remembered Toothacker as he saw him now, with his nose in a bottle.

Somewhere in the back of Alvarez's mind a voice told him to stand a little straighter himself, to take extra care walking after the whiskey. Toothacker, above all other men he knew, was living testament to Alvarez's code that drinking and lawing didn't mix. "He's drunk already," he said, being careful to keep his own words from slurring.

"Not already. Still. Sure as hell is a good thing we won't see any action tonight, ain't it?" Comstock laughed so hard it brought tears to his eyes.

Tom Alvarez realized his right leg hurt worse than ever.

Chapter 3

THE DISTINGUISHED GENTLEMAN AND HIS COMPANION sat in the carriage down the street from the big gray house. Nothing set it apart from all the other houses along the street except, perhaps, a gloomy somberness that pervaded the place. The huge, twisted cottonwood in the yard had prematurely shed its leaves and its gnarled limbs and branches were beckoning and sinister.

The man from out of town smiled and puffed deeply on his cigar, allowing the smoke to curl and gather in a little blue cloud under the narrow rim of his black derby. He thrust his fat fingers into the pocket of his vest and extracted the watch.

"You have made all the proper arrangements?"

His companion nodded. "Yes."

"Excellent."

"Before we proceed, though, sir, you ought to consider the consequences very carefully," his companion said carefully.

Angered by this insolence, the gentleman clenched his

teeth and nearly bit the cigar in two. He saw the fleeting trace of fear dance across the other man's eyes, and it pleased him.

"What consequences?" His voice was detached and utterly emotionless. He snapped open the watch case, read the time while he waited for an answer, and snapped it shut.

The other man cleared his throat. "There may be political matters to deal with," he said delicately. "The woman has… some importance in our community.

Blue smoke drifted from the glowing end of the cigar. "The woman is a common whore, and you will kindly let me worry about political consequences. That is my business, after all."

"Still, you should give careful consideration—"

The gentleman cut him short. "There will be no conesquences. Not if this job is properly done. I assume you have seen to that?"

"Of course, but—"

"No buts. It will be properly done and there will be no consequences. It is quite as simple as that. Do I make myself perfectly clear?"

The other man swallowed once before answering, as if he had something in his throat that he was having difficulty getting down. "Yes. It's just that I wish I had your confidence."

The gentleman smiled vaguely, condescendingly. "Frankly, it doesn't matter whether you are confident or not. I'm a man of details and exactitude, and I have spent a great deal of time considering all aspects of this matter. If it is carried out according to my specific plan, it quite simply cannot fail." He smiled around the black stub of the cigar, but his eyes were had and cold, and he dropped the next words into the stillness between them like stones into a quiet pool. "Only if someone fails to do his job can anything go wrong, and you assure me you have taken great pains to see to it that that doesn't happen." The smile widened, showing yellow teeth.

The companion wiped beads of perspiration from his forehead, even though it was cool in the carriage. "I've taken great pains, yes," he repeated.

"And you can depend on your man?"

"Yes… absolutely."

"You hesitate. Can you depend on him or not?"

"Absolutely."

The gentleman stretched out one arm and folded his fingers to examine his buffed and perfectly trimmed nails. "Excellent." He leaned back in his seat. "Well, then, perhaps we'd best be on our way. Until the proper time."

The companion leaned forward to signal the driver with his walking stick, but the gentleman caught the stick and hand together in an iron grip.

"I am deadly serious about this," he said. "You tell me everything is arranged and I am forced to believe you. But there will be no mistakes."

"None, sir," the other said.

The gentleman smiled again and released the hand. "Excellent. Excellent!" He raised his voice only slightly. "Driver, let us be on our way!"

At the command, the driver drew the reins tight and flicked them over the heads of the matched team of gray geldings. The carriage lurched into motion and rolled down the street, passing the dark whorehouse and crunching through the litter of decaying leathery cottonwood leaves before turning up a side street that connected with the boulevard that would carry them back into the heart of the city.

Chapter 4

ARNOLD TOOTHACKER TOOK A DEEP BREATH to steady himself before he dared pass through the double-wide doorway into the great ballroom. Uniformed waiters carrying big silver trays loaded with dirty dishes gave him sour looks as the hurried past, but he scarcely saw them. His mouth was cotton-dry and he already needed another drink. He rubbed the back of his hand across his cheeks. Although he'd shaved before dinner, he'd had such a case of the shakes he'd just about botched it; even now, several hours later, sticky blood still gathered in the deepest nicks.

The noise coming from the ballroom had the boom and roll of some strange slow-motion explosion: thundering male voices, deep belly laughs, hoarse voices raised in an old song, the pounding of fists on linen-covered tabletops, and the sharper higher-pitched sounds of rattling silverware and clinking crystal all assaulted his ears.

He stared into the smoky bowels of the room, trying to find Tom Alvarez and Ben Comstock in the crowd, but he'd lost them. Or more likely, they were avoiding him. Not that he particularly blamed them. It was something he'd become accustomed to in recent years.

He crossed the threshold into the ballroom.

A waiter with a tray of brandy snifters scurried past him and swung around in the general direction of a knot of men where Bill Cody was busy holding court.

Toothacker licked his dry lips. God, how he needed a drink. Worse than he needed his friends.

He followed the waiter.

Now that dinner and the formal welcoming speeches were behind them, Buffalo Bill had taken what passed for center stage in the middle of the room, and he was clearly in his glory spinning yarns of derring-do and Indian wars and buffalo hunting days to anyone who would listen. Cody was resplendent in flowing gray-streaked brown hair and goatee and buckskins: his glove-tanned and sueded shirt glittered with carefully stitched beadwork, new yellow trousers were tucked into the tops of polished thigh-high riding boots, and long fringed gloves decorated with geometric designs of porcupine quills were folded over a red sash belt. Even among these men, who knew most of Cody's exploits were pure balderdash invented by Ned Buntline to thrill New York theatergoers thirty years before, there were plenty who were nonetheless eager to hear the tall tales once more; as always, Cody's most outrageous lies had a magical quality about them that could mesmerize the most cynical old-timer. And if ever the exploits did begin to lose their power, Cody was crafty enough to slip into truer (and just as wondrous) tales of kings and princes and European castles and courtyards. Rumors that Cody and his Wild West Show were on the verge of financial collapse were always making the rounds, but Colonel William F. Cody always put on a good show, even if he was down to his last dime.

Toothacker eased himself alongside the tight cluster of men just as Cody and his party snatched up the last of the brandies from the tray. Cody gave him a toothy grin, swept him into the group with a theatrical gesture, and draped an arm and one soft, uncalloused hand over Toothacker's shoulder. Cody smelled of good whiskey and cheap toilet water.

"Arnold, old friend, I was just telling these boys about the time I introduced Sitting Bull to the queen of England." Bill cast a practiced eye around the crowd to make sure they were listening. "I swear it was the only time in his life the red bastard was impressed by a white person. Old Sit, he'd spent half his life trying to get his people to the safety of the 'Grandmother's Land' of Canada, and when I told him Her Majesty was the grandmother herself, he was quite beside himself. He actually bowed!" Cody mimicked Sitting Bull by screwing up his face and nodded his head stiffly.

The men who were gathered around laughed appreciatively at the story.

"Kind of hard to believe old Sit would bow to anyone," Toothacker said skeptically, and even before the words were out, he was sorry he'd said it.

Cody's eyes flashed with sudden anger, then softened just as quickly with the unmistakable look of profound pity. "Hard but true, Arnold, hard but true," he said.

Toothacker tried to smile.

"Ah, well," Cody said, and in a heartbeat he'd turned his attention to the other men. By the time Toothacker squirmed out from under Buffalo Bill's arm, Cody was well into another old chestnut about the time he'd guided the

Grand Duke Alexis on a buffalo hunt.

Toothacker searched in vain for something to drink; he'd heard that one a thousand times. It never varied an iota, as if it were from some memorized script. But then, it probably was. With Cody, you could never be sure. Part of the old fraud's charm lay in his ability to wring applause from the same material year after year. And how it worked! The men gathered around were under the old scout's spell already, even though each and every one of them claimed to hold him in contempt—had, in fact, said vile things about him when they found out he would dare to appear with them this very same evening.

William Frederick Cody was somehow larger than life.

And Arnold Toothacker was going in the other direction.

He sat down a little apart from the knot of men.

He'd been a good lawman once, one of the best in Colorado and western Kansas, earning his reputation by bringing law and order almost singlehandedly to forty thousand square miles of frontier in his time. Then, like Cody, he'd managed to live on that reputation for an additional twenty years. Now his string was up.

At bottom, the problem was simple. Liquor was killing him. He'd fought against the bottle for a quarter century, and it had won, as he'd known all along it would. Even as he sat listening to old Bill, he ached for a shot of rye. He'd slipped away from the banquet to toss back a couple of quick shots in the bar, just because they weren't pouring in the ballroom until the speeches were finished, and if he was honest with himself, he had to admit he'd come back now only because they were handing out the brandy and cigars. He didn't care a thing about the smokes, but a drink of some kind would soon be as necessary as the air he breathed.

He focused on the tablecloth in front of him. Butter and breadcrumbs were scattered about, and it was stained with gravy and port wine. He flicked idly at the crumbs with his thumb.

Dinner had been a disaster. He'd made it a point to sit with Ben Comstock and Tom Alvarez, his oldest comrades, in spite of the hostile reception they'd given him. The two men he'd worked with most closely back in the glory days were hardly civil to him now. Comstock talked as much as ever, but it was all one-sided chatter, and he kept his hooded eyes averted from Toothacker as if he were embarrassed to look him in the face. Alvarez—whom Toothacker admired more than any other man on earth for his flinty honest and intelligence—merely sat in stone-faced silence, his hawk nose turned away in disgust.

Toothacker tried to remember the first time he and Comstock and Alvarez had worked together. It had been a train robbery, he thought. Back around '77 or '78. But he couldn't recall any of the specifics, and the harder he tried, the hazier it became.

He did remember clearly that there had been a time when the three of them had been closer than any other men in the service. Of course, they'd been competitors, too, with each trying to outdo the other, make the most arrests, recover the most contraband, do the best job of tracking in a trackless country. They'd never been close friends in the usual sense of the word, because men in their line of work weren't given to such intimacy, but their dedication to duty had been a bond far stronger than mere friendship ever could have been. But now that bond was broken; neither

Comstock nor Alvarez wanted anything to do with him. He'd spilled more than Alvarez had drunk, and when the speeches began and he'd gotten up to sneak out to the bar, he'd heard them sigh with relief.

A waiter came by with a tray full of brandy snifters and humidor of cigars, and Arnold Toothacker took a drink and tossed most of it down. The brandy was smooth, with a pleasant bite to it, but he hardly noticed: his taste in liquor had deteriorated in direct proportion to his need for it. He stared into the bottom of the glass, studying the way the golden drops of liquor flowed together like oil, while the camaraderie in the great room ebbed and flowed around him without taking him in.

He was startled when a large hand clamped down on his shoulder. It was Bill Tilghman.

"I seen you come in, Arnold." Tilghman smiled, the corners of his thin mouth curling up beneath the scraggly mustache. "You all right?"

Toothacker faked a smile in return.

"Ben Comstock was at your table, wasn't he? That sumbitch owes me a brandy or two." Tilghman's grin widened.

Toothacker felt himself sag a little in the chair as if he had no control over his own body. "I… haven't seen him in a while, Bill. I stepped out."

Tilghman clapped his shoulder again. "Oh, well. Thanks. If you do see him, tell him I was lookin' for him," he said as he moved away, nodding and laughing with the other old-timers as he went.

Toothacker rose unsteadily and waited for the rubber to leave his legs, then shoved off, steering for the exit. He suddenly needed the quiet of the bar. The big double doors to the lobby seemed a mile away.

Another hand caught his arm. It was Cody.

"Whoa, hoss. You ain't leaving us?" The old scout's blue eyes sparkled.

"I… need some air," Arnold stammered. The lie came out more a whimper than anything else. He wiped at his dry lips again.

"Looks like you need a drink, hoss." Cody winked, and the waxed ends of his white mustache notched upward above the surprisingly good mouth. "A breath of fresh air beforehand might be just the ticket. Mind if I come along?"

Arnold shook his head.

Cody retrieved his yellow doeskin jacket from a nearby table, pulled it on with a flourish, then swept himself and Arnold Toothacker through the doors, across the lobby, and into the street in front of the hotel.

Ben Comstock took a small sip from the brandy snifter. His eyes narrowed almost imperceptibly toward the wide double doors across the room. "Look there."

Tom Alvarez sighed and exhaled a cloud of blue cigar smoke. "Those two old fakers belong together," he said through his teeth.

The night was cool, the air faintly scented with wood smoke and horse dung. Cody struck up a conversation with the doorman and, with the unerring instincts of a natural showman, positioned himself perfectly under the gaslight so he'd be seen by hotel guests and any passersby out for an evening drive. Toothacker slumped against the brick façade of the building, but Cody reached out a fancy beaded gauntlet and pulled him gently from the shadows.

"Clarence, my good man," Cody said, addressing the doorman, "this is none other than Arnold Prescott Toothacker, the most renowned lawman in the history of the fair state of Colorado. Such establishments as yours would never have risen from the prairie sod if it hadn't been for men like Marshal Toothacker. His ceaseless efforts to bring peace to the frontier were a source of pride for all of us who played a role in western settlement!"

The doorman smirked at Cody's bombast. "I've heard of Marshal Toothacker."

"We needed a breath of air," Toothacker said weakly.

Cody tipped his head back and drew in a lungful of the cool evening air through his Roman nose. "This night has the very scent of adventure about it, don't you think, gentlemen?"

Clarence giggled. "Smells like horseshit to me, Colonel."

Cody let out a great booming, theatrical laugh. "Yes, well, I do believe that says it succinctly!" he roared with genuine good humor. "Perhaps, Clarence, you could raise a hansom cab for Marshal Toothacker and me so we might do homage to the ladies of Denver this fine night."

Clarence snickered again, but bowed politely just the same. "Absolutely, Colonel Cody." He swept to the curb and waved a white-gloved hand in the air. From somewhere out of the darkness came a whistle, the stirring of dozing horses, and the clip-clop and rumble of horseshoes and iron tires on brick pavement. The cab rolled to a stop at the curb, and Clarence opened the door and beckoned the two gentlemen inside.

Toothacker climbed aboard and let Cody take care of the directions and the tip for the doorman.

"I trust you are in the mood for a little sport this evening?" Cody said, settling onto the leather seat next to him.

Toothacker could only see the wisp of white goatee and long yellow-white hair and faint glow of the doeskin jacket in the darkness of the hansom; somehow he'd lost the thread of what was happening, wasn't even quite sure now why he'd left the hotel with Cody.

"Sport?" he asked after a time.

Cody chuckled. "Woman, Arnold! Women!" Cody patted him on the knee with a fringed gauntlet, much as he might a favorite dog.

With a sigh, Toothacker settled deeper into the soft leather.

The hansom rumbled over the cobblestones. Clouds of fluttering autumn insects choked the pools of light around the gas lamps, and nighthawks darted in and out of the clouds, feasting on the plenty. Men in paper collars and neckties stood in front of the better saloons with brandy snifters in their hands and good cigars clenched between their teeth; at the dives, rumpled, mustachioed men in grimy miners' caps pitched dice in makeshift craps pits, their faces softly lit by the red glow of roll-your-own cigarettes. The hansom left the downtown area, rolled past the capitol and on toward south Denver, where fancy brick homes gave way to smaller frame dwellings on tiny lots, in turn giving way to row on row of identical clapboard bungalows. The street lamps did not extend into this part of the city, and only white moonlight and the dull orange glow shining through oilcloth-draped windows gave form to the houses. They passed a Catholic church; Toothacker could make out the brightly colored madonna painted on one wall. The *barrio*, he thought. The melancholy sound of a guitar playing a Mexican love song drifted on the night air, and a little shiver ran up his spine. He had a strange sensation that he was being watched by ghosts.

He felt very old and tired. And very dry.

"You wouldn't have a flask on you, would you, Bill?" he asked.

Cody chuckled and reached into the beautiful jacket and produced a silver-plated half-pint flask, which he handed over.

"Purely for medicinal purposes, now, Arnold."

"Purely." Toothacker wrenched off the cap and held the bottle to his lips. It was sour-mash whiskey, very good. The liquor trickled down his throat, and he felt the power of it calming his nerves instantly. He took a second swallow and handed back the flask.

Cody took a swig himself and screwed on the cap.

The hansom turned up a side street and moved west toward the river and a clutter of brick warehouses. A mosquito buzzed around their heads and Cody swatted at it, missing.

"Damnable things," Cody said, mostly to himself. "I remember a swarm of skeeters so bad along the Belle Fourche they like to drove the horses crazy. Indians never were bothered, though, nor their ponies, neither. Smelled too bad, I'd reckon. Skeeters like the clean smell of a white man."

They were past the warehouses now, very near the river. The driver turned south again, and they came to a row of aging frame homes falling into decay. He pulled up and stopped under the twisted branches of a huge cottonwood in front of the largest of the dark, peeling houses. It was a three-story affair with ornate gables over the upper windows, turrets on the corners, and a wide porch that ran the width of the house and curled around a portion of the south side as well. The windows glowed dull red in the darkness; heavy velvet curtains shielded the interior from prying eyes.

Cody stepped down, alighting on the stone curb much more gracefully than his years or weight should have permitted. Toothacker followed. A scrawny yellow dog loped across a weedy vacant lot, barked once, and disappeared down an alley.

"You'll wait for us, my good man?" Cody asked the driver. "It'll be worth ten dollars."

The man whistled in appreciation and doffed his hat.

"The mistress here is a first-class woman," Cody whispered to Toothacker as he led the way across the weedy yard. He strode across the porch, ignoring the creak of weathered boards, lifted the heavy brass doorknocker, and brought it down three times on the strikeplate. He paused, then knocked twice more.

"It's a code," he said. "Only the best of Madam's clientele are permitted entrance at this time of evening—and only those who know the code."

Toothacker nodded dumbly and waited for the door to open. "It's been years since I visited a whorehouse," he said, recognizing how thin the lie sounded. "Since before I married Gertrude, at least." That sounded even less convincing, and thought of Gertrude—stern, strong, long-suffering Gertrude—made him ache all the more for another drink.

"Every married man needs a little sport now and again," Cody offered grandly. "Why, I myself—" He was interruptted by the low groan of the door swinging open.

Yellow lamplight spilled onto the porch, silhouetting a small man whose torso appeared twisted by some deformity of the spine.

"Good evening, Colonel Cody! How charming to see you again!" The man's voice was marvelously deep and rich in spite of his size, with the softness of the South to it. "Madam will be pleased to see you, sir!"

"Ulysses, my good man, how nice to see you as well," Cody said with exaggerated gallantry as he stepped across the threshold.

Ulysses closed the door carefully after them and led them down a long green-carpeted hallway. He appeared to be thirty or maybe younger. It struck Toothacker as strange to find such an imperfect creature in the ornate setting of the brothel, but in spite of the man's deformity, there was a grace and power in the way he walked; it didn't take much effort to imagine this bent figure manhandling unruly guests with ease.

The man stopped in front of the heavy mahogany sliding door into the parlor, drew himself up to his greatest height, and slid it open.

"Madam, Colonel William Frederick Cody and a friend!" He bowed slightly as he announced them, then allowed the two men to proceed into the room. The door slid shut behind them.

Several gentlemen, lounging around the room on ornate divans, and a half-dozen scantily clad young women stared at the great Buffalo Bill. Cody gave them his most winning smile, swept off his high-crowned Stetson, and bowed to the waist, his long hair falling about his face and then back into place as he rose. Two of the women applauded daintily and several of the gentlemen, suddenly uncomfortable in the presence of someone as famous as the showman, cleared their throats nervously or busied themselves with their drinks. Only the hostess, ensconced on a pile of velvet pillows, seemed unimpressed. She rose slowly, steadying herself with the gleaming ebony cane, and adjusted the sedate black dress that covered her full bosom. Toothacker saw that she was crippled, with a withered leg and arm. She gave them a looking over, then tossed her head back, threatening to loosen a pile of fiery red-dyed tresses, and laughed out loud in Cody's face.

"William, my handsome friend, it's been a long time since I've welcomed you to my parlor!" Her voice was strong and sure, a commanding voice very like Gertrude Toothacker's.

"You look as lovely as ever, my dear!" Cody said as he bowed and kissed her hand. "Maggie, let me introduce Arnold Toothacker, marshal from Pueblo." His arm swept back in an arc and pulled Toothacker forward. "Arnold, meet Margaret Corcoran. Mrs. Corcoran is this fair city's best businesswoman. Damned if she may not be the best anywhere!"

Toothacker held out his hand and Margaret Corcoran took it. Her grip was firm.

"I've heard a good many things about you, Marshal," she said.

Toothacker blushed without being quite sure why. "Yes, ma'am," he said.

"I have a new girl working for me from Pueblo. Lillian is her name. A lovely child. Perhaps you know her." She gave him a broad smile that conveyed nothing and let his hand slip from her fingers. "One of my girls will bring you a brandy, or we have whiskey if you prefer." She swept a hand around the room. "As you can see, brandy seems to be the drink of choice this evening."

Toothacker blushed again and wiped the back of his hands across his lips. Something she'd said worked in his mind, but he couldn't quite keep track of it. He was so damned dry. "A brandy would be fine."

Margaret Corcoran nodded to one of the scantily clad girls, who hurried through a small side door. She then turned her back on Toothacker, took Cody by the arm, and steered him toward her throne of velvet pillows, using him instead of the cane for support.

By the time the drinks arrived, Cody had already divested himself of his fringed jacket, and one of the girls was pulling at his thigh-high boots. The other guests, seeing that the great man was intent on his own pleasures, returned to theirs.

Arnold Toothacker took a swallow of brandy and retreated to one end of an empty divan.

Mrs. Corcoran looked over at him. "Marshal, I'll fetch Lillian for you if you wish. Or you can go to her room at the back of the house."

Toothacker took another swallow. His glass was already empty, much too soon. Lillian. *Lillian.* "That would be fine," he stammered.

"Which? Her room?"

"Fine."

Margaret Corcoran gave him the tiniest of curtsies and hobbled to the sliding doors, opened them just wide enough to slip out, and was gone.

"Mrs. Corcoran's is as grand a house as there is, Arnold!" Cody said expansively as he pulled one of the girls down to him and gave her a kiss on the lips. She giggled like a schoolgirl. "There's no better sport anywhere."

Toothacker stared at his empty glass and waited.

In a few moments, Mrs. Corcoran returned with Ulysses, who bowed slightly.

Toothacker rose and followed.

The house was huge and unusually long front to back, with numerous rooms off the main hallway and a second darker hallway perpendicular to the first running the length of a single-story addition across the rear. Dark oil paintings of scenes from mythology lined the walls. Single beeswax candles on marble-topped tables beneath the oils provided the only illumination, and the air was heavy with the sweet smells of perfume and mildew.

Ulysses led the way to a door at the far end of the second hall, rapped once, then turned and strode past Arnold without so much as a nod of the head.

"Sir," Toothacker called after him.

The man stopped.

"Could I have… something to drink? Some rye whiskey, perhaps?"

Ulysses nodded once with a thin smile and disappeared into the gloom.

Toothacker heard the door open behind him and turned to face it. The soft light coming from within was only marginally brighter than the light in the hallway; it was at once restful and sinister. He peered into the room but saw no one. Then fingers, long and white, curled around the edge of the door and pulled it open wider, revealing a slender young woman in a white satin gown, standing just beyond the doorframe.

"Come in," she said in a throaty voice, then her eyes met his with a blink of recognition. Her long fingers went to her mouth in surprise.

He gulped. "Lilly Morgan," he said so quietly the sound seemed to come from someone else.

"Hello, Arnold," she said so softly he barely heard her. She backed away from him with a sensuous, fluid motion that didn't quite beckon him, yet drew him into the room and toward her with a power he couldn't resist.

She lowered herself onto the edge of the bed in the center of the room with the same careless, natural grace that had tormented him in his dreams, and it made his heart ache.

"Well," Toothacker said, and his voice cracked on the single word. He hoped the hunchback would hurry with the liquor. He needed it desperately.

"Well," she repeated softly. "How have you been, Arnold?" She crossed her legs, and the white satin slipped off her ankle and calf, revealing a slim leg of milky color.

He had never seen her look so beautiful.

"Fine, Lilly. Fine."

She smiled at him with a genuine tenderness that took his breath away, and for a heartbeat their eyes met again. Hers were deep and brown and soft, very much like the eyes of a frightened deer, but even as he watched, the softness and life ebbed away, leaving only emptiness.

"How are you?" he asked.

"I'm perfect, Arnold," she said. "You look well."

"No, I don't."

She threw her head back and let out a surprisingly harsh laugh that made her sound far older than she was. "Whatever you say, love. I always did admire your honesty. Now, let's get down to business. What can I do for you tonight?"

Chapter 5

TOM ALVAREZ SHIFTED HIS WEIGHT onto his good leg. God, how he wished this evening would end. It was past midnight and felt even later. The incessant drone of loud conversation, the various animal sounds of older men who had eaten and drunk too much, even the clinking of glassware and the scrape of chairs and boots on the parquet floor had, along with the wine, given him a splitting headache. He scowled at Ben Comstock in the vain hope that Ben would take the hint and end this argument about Pat Garrett's last days.

"Shot the poor bastard in the back," Comstock was saying for the fourth or fifth time. "Poor old Pat was standing there beside the wagon, taking a leak, and that sonofabitch Wayne Brazel let him have it right in the back of the head. He was dead before he hit the ground."

One of the others Alvarez didn't recognize snorted. "Some say it served him right, goin' like that. He never give some others a sportin' chance, includin' the Kid."

Comstock's hooded eyes nearly closed, a flush of anger

came to his face, but he let it pass and only raised his brandy snifter as if to study the golden liquor. There was a good swallow, and he swirled it around once before tossing it down. "If any of us was in the business of givin' criminals a *sporting* chance, we would've been dead years ago."

"I always believed in givin' the other fellas a chance," the other man said.

Comstock set his glass down carefully. "Then you're a damn fool. A lucky one, but a fool just the same."

The other man bristled at the insult and took a menacing step toward Comstock, but Alvarez managed to slide in between them.

"So what happened to Brazel, Ben?" Alvarez gave Comstock's adversary what he hoped was a disarming smile. It was too damn late and his head hurt too badly to get mixed up in a fight now.

Comstock looked back into the brandy glass, as if he expected to find something in it. "Oh, the sonofabitch got off scot free," he said. "There was a trial, but he was acquitted. Far's I'm concerned, some of Pat's old enemies from as far back as the Albert Jennings Fountain business bought and paid for that acquittal, though I can't prove it."

"I head some talk that Billy the Kid's still alive an' mebbe he had a han' in Garrett's death," one of the other men said.

Comstock laughed the dry, cruel laugh he'd once been famous for, the laugh that made the hair stand up on the back of a grown man's neck. "Some damn idjit or another's been sayin' the Kid's alive for the last thirty goddamn years. It ain't true."

Damn, Alvarez thought. Here we go again.

"I've heard talk is all," the other man said.

"Talk's cheap. I know fifty men claim to have seen him, an' there's one old woman up in Las Cruces says she lived with him in Juarez back in the nineties. 'Nother old boy over to Roswell says the Kid's still a workin' cowhand in east Texas, an' I've even heard it said ol' John Chisum's niece Sally visits the Kid once or twice a year in Mexico. If you ask me, it's all pure horsefeathers. I knew Pat Garrett as well as any man alive, an' when he says he killed Billy Bonney, I believe him. Ol' Pat had his enemies, but the worst enemy he ever had wouldn't call him a liar." Comstock let out the laugh again. "At least not to his face."

Alvarez shifted his weight again and looked at his pocketwatch. It was almost one o'clock. The endless jabbering had been going on for over five hours, and from the looks of things, it could go on for five more. "Point is, Pat's dead at the hand of a scoundrel, and that's that. So let's leave him be."

The other men agreed with that, at least. They'd all had enemies, and they'd had plenty of friends down through the years who'd gone to their graves the way Garrett had; when all was said and done, the only thing that separated the dead from the living was a measure of luck.

Comstock's hooded eyes opened a little wider and he gave Alvarez what passed for a little half-smile. "Then let's all drink to ol' Patrick," he said, and he moved to flag down a bartender.

Alvarez sighed and excused himself to find a toilet.

The men's lavatory was off to the side of the lobby, and when he finished he found a green satin wingback chair with an ottoman where he could rest his foot. The chair was so new the upholstery hadn't yet turned black from hair pomade, and it reminded him of his own favorite chair at home, with the sunken seat that fit his body perfectly and the dark stains on the back in spite of the clean doilies his wife kept pinned to the back and both arms. His body ached with fatigue, and he knew he should go up to bed, but he didn't have the energy to make the long climb up the stairs. He settled into the chair and squirmed around, trying to get comfortable, and closed his eyes.

This evening of old war stories had worn him down. The fellows who embellished their tales of bygone days were living in the past, and he prided himself on living in the present. Which, when he considered it, made him wonder again why he'd come to Denver, why he'd subjected himself to all this. Maybe it was some old sense of responsibility to these men who'd shared the dangers of his profession and had helped establish—for good or ill—the rule of law throughout the West. Perhaps it was just plain old-fashioned curiosity, a hankering to see how these boys had aged in the last twenty years.

Or, perhaps, his wife was right. She'd said he was pining for the old days himself and needed to recount the old adventures one more time before he could let them go. He'd grumbled at her and told her she didn't know what she was talking about, but if he was honest with himself, he guessed she was on the right track after all. Maybe it was his own stories he wanted to hear instead of others' tales.

He fidgeted some more until he found a position that was fairly comfortable, and within moments he drifted off to sleep.

When someone tapped him lightly on the shoulder, he jumped and twisted around to see who it was. A slight man with slicked-back dark hair and eyes that matched the gray wool of his tailored suit gave him a little bow. He appeared to be somewhere in his early forties, twenty years younger than most of the conventioneers.

"Excuse me for asking you, but aren't you Marshal Thomas Alvarez from Abilene?" the gentleman asked.

Alvarez nodded.

The small man thrust out a white, well-manicured hand. When Alvarez shook it, he found the grip surprisingly strong.

"I'm Theodore Paine," the man said.

"Pleased to meet you."

"I'm commissioner of police for the city of Denver," Paine said. "I've been enjoying the companionship of your friends this evening."

Alvarez recognized him now. Paine had been at the head table, and he'd been introduced with some other local dignitaries before the after-dinner speeches began. Alvarez indicated another wingback chair. He longed to be left alone, but he'd made it a habit never to ignore a police commissioner in a city as large as Denver, and the old habits died hard.

Pain pulled the chair closer with the easy grace of a man very much at home with strangers. "My apologies. I don't want to intrude. It's just that I've been an admirer of yours for some years."

Alvarez stifled a yawn. The compliment sounded sincere.

Pain tapped a finger on a vest pocket. "Care for a cigar? I happen to have two Havanas I've been saving."

Alvarez found himself grinning. "Absolutely." If he was going to be saddled with unwanted company, at least he could enjoy the spicy taste of Cuban tobacco.

The two men took their time with the formalities of

clipping the ends and lighting their cigars. The pungent smoke curled around their heads, and they remained silent until the heavy ashes on the Havanas were an inch long.

"Excellent," Paine said appreciatively, as he let the ash fall into the cuspidor at his feet. "A good smoke is one of life's great pleasures, don't you think?"

Alvarez agreed. "But you have me at a disadvantage, sir. You claim to be an admirer of mine. How so?"

Pain drew in a mouthful of aromatic smoke and released it slowly. "I'm originally from Lawrence, Kansas. Moved here fifteen years ago. I was an inspector at the federal prison in Leavenworth for several years back in the early nineties, and I was aware of your remarkable record with the U. S. Marshal's service."

Alvarez couldn't keep a small smile of embarrassment from cracking the corner of his mouth. "I will admit I sent more than a few young men to Leavenworth."

"Those you brought in alive seldom won acquittal, as I recall."

Alvarez waved it off. "Good judges saw to that."

"Good judges can't do their jobs without good policework. You paved the way for the rest of us, Marshal."

"The name's Tom, Commissioner."

"Tom. And you may call me Ted."

Alvarez smiled warmly, feeling much better suddenly in such civilized company. "Ted," he said easily.

The two smoked and talked of good policework, and when the cigars were half gone, they retired to the bar at Paine's suggestion. Alvarez ordered only sparkling water for a nightcap, and the commissioner did the same.

Other old-timers drifted into the bar as the festivities in the ballroom wound down, and Alvarez introduced Paine to them. Although the commissioner spoke warmly to each in turn, Alvarez was pleased and flattered to note that he never told them he admired them; judging from first impressions, Paine was a lawman in the old mold, one whose flinty honesty more than made up for the expensive clothes and manicured hands. As they chatted, Alvarez noted that the commissioner sipped his plain seltzer slowly and carefully, as if it were as strong as the brandy they'd had so much of earlier. Habit, Alvarez thought with pleasure; habits like that made for good policework.

"A man in our line of work is well served by avoiding strong drink," Alvarez observed, and he lifted his seltzer in a toast to his new friend.

"Absolutely," Paine agreed, hoisting his own glass.

Ben Comstock found them a half hour later and pulled up a chair without being invited. Alvarez made the formal introductions. "Ben's a former marshal from—"

"From El Paso," Paine said at once, and he extended his hand. "I've heard a great deal about Marshal Comstock down through the years. I'm Theodore Paine."

Comstock gave the proffered hand a sloppy shake. "G'd evenin', sir," he said, his voice thickened to a slur. "Glad you could spen' some time with us ol' farts!" He laughed too loudly at his own crudity and waved awkwardly at a waiter. "Bourbon whiskey, sir! I need one more 'fore I turn in."

"The liquor's quite good in this establishment, isn't it?" Paine said evenly, looking at Alvarez.

"Damn good," Comstock agreed. "Goes to the head." He giggled and started to say something else, but forgot what it was.

Pain turned his attention back to Alvarez. "You'll have to stop by my headquarters and see our layout," he said easily. "It has all the latest equipment. Law enforcement is really becoming quite scientific nowadays. You'd be surprised at some of the techniques of modern detective work."

"All we ever had was our wits," Alvarez offered. "Usually, it was all we needed." There was no false modesty in the statement.

"You're absolutely correct," Paine agreed. "That's what's so amazing to me. If you'd had the scientific knowledge that we have at our disposal now, you'd have been able to do so much more. I dare say, the frontier would have been rid of crime twenty years earlier than it was."

Comstock snorted. "Who says the frontier's rid of crime now? There's a hell of a lot of crime in west Texas, I'll tell you that."

"Of course there are still areas where ruffians abound, Marshal," Paine said politely. "I was speaking of the more civilized parts of our region."

"Such as Denver," Comstock said icily.

Paine nodded while deliberately keeping his eyes averted. "Yes. Such as Denver."

Alvarez saw the hot blood come to Comstock's face again, and he held up a hand wearily. Scratch beneath the surface, and Ben Comstock was still a combative old bastard. "Please, gentlemen. Let's not argue." He wasn't used to being a peacemaker, and it seemed he'd done little else this evening.

Comstock took the hint reluctantly; he tossed down his whiskey without taking his eyes off the commissioner and mumbled an apology.

After what seemed like a long time, Paine smiled and

lifted his glass in the slightest toast to Ben Comstock.

"My apologies, as well, Marshal," he said evenly. "Sometimes I forget that parts of this country are still half-wild."

The sky was just turning the faintest gray when the sharp knock came at Alvarez's door. He was instantly awake out of a lifetime of habit, but once again it took him too long to remember where he was. He groaned in disgust and crawled out of bed; he'd been asleep less than two hours.

"Who is it?" His throat was raspy and he felt his pulse in his temples. He couldn't remember the last time he'd been hung over.

Whoever it was knocked again.

"I said, who the hell is it?"

The response came through the closed door clearly. "Ted Paine, Thomas. Sorry to wake you."

Alvarez stood up, putting weight gingerly on his bad leg. The bone ached deep inside. Pulling on an old robe, he tottered across the room and opened the door.

"I'm sorry," Paine said. "Seems as if all I do is wake you up." He looked as fresh and alert as if he'd had a full night's sleep. "Duty calls, I'm afraid. There's been a murder in one of the more unsavory houses a few miles from here." Alvarez noticed a certain lack of color in Paine's face. "One or two of our local businessmen have been detained for questioning, and it takes a deft and knowing touch."

Alvarez pulled his robe tighter. "What can I do?"

Paine studied his shoes, as if in embarrassment. "It seems one of your old friends is involved. Trouble is, the gentleman is of some repute here in Colorado as well."

"One of my friends?" Alvarez scratched his head.

Paine didn't lift his eyes. "It's Arnold Toothacker."

"Dead?" Alvarez's jaw dropped.

Paine shuffled his feet nervously. "No. He's our principal suspect."

Chapter 6

Tom Alvarez stood on the iron runway in front of the cell and shook his head. Arnold Toothacker was the sorriest-looking human being Alvarez had seen in years. The old man's chest heaved as he sat on the tattered mattress inside the cell, his head buried in his hands, seemingly oblivious to the dried blood and vomit on his rumpled suit.

A cockroach scurried out from under the iron cot where Toothacker sat, then ran across the toe of his shoe and out under the cell door. Alvarez waited for the insect and stomped his foot where he thought it would be, but it was too fast for him: he had to watch as it scuttled down the runway and disappeared into a crack in the damp brick wall.

"Come on, Arnold. The cavalry's come for you," Alvarez said, and wished immediately he'd made it sound kinder. The old man was in a bad enough state without the added burden of sarcasm from an old acquaintance. But then again, Alvarez reminded himself, he shouldn't be too soft, either. Why should he go easy on a man who'd kept him away from a hearty breakfast and a well-deserved rest—and had, perhaps, committed a murder into the bargain?

"Arnold, let's go," Alvarez said again, a little louder this time.

Toothacker looked up. His eyes were bloodshot and puffy and he had a painful-looking deep bruise along his left cheek. He squinted as if trying to see who it was that had spoken. Recognition crept slowly across his battered face. "Oh. Hello, Tom."

"Got yourself in a hell of a fix, Arnold."

Toothacker scratched his head and looked down at his soiled shirt without answering. A hell of a fix, all right, he thought.

He studied his hands, saw the dried blood, and tried to remember. Was it hours ago, or days? Something about a woman. And then it came to him…

The oak-and-satin chair engulfed Toothacker, threatening to drown him in its soft, suffocating opulence as he downed one drink after another. Lilly Morgan reclined on the bed a few feet away, and no matter how hard he tried, he couldn't escape the unbearable pressure of her brown deer-eyes. Thankfully, the whiskey was very good: he poured himself a third drink. Or was it the fourth? He'd already lost count, and his head was buzzing.

"You look… well," she repeated after a time.

"So do you." He, at least, was telling the truth. She was the loveliest thing he had ever seen. Always had been, and the passage of time had only made her lovelier. Her skin was almost as white as the silken canopy over her bed and at least as smooth; even across the room, even with the smell of the liquor in his nose, he caught her scent, and it was the same as always—the scent of pure soap and sweet herbs and the faintest trace of womanhood.

"I thought you were going to San Francisco," he said, not really surprised at how much nerve it took to ask such a simple question.

"I was," she said and tossed her head, shaking the dark curls, making them shimmer in the lamplight. "I changed my mind."

He couldn't tell whether there was sadness or resignation in her voice. Perhaps both. Or neither.

"You should have gone to San Francisco. It would have been better for you than Denver."

"Why?"

He thought for a moment. Why, indeed? "The air's better," he said at last. "They say the sea air is a tonic for all sorts of physical complaints."

She let out a little mechanical laugh that made the gooseflesh stand on his neck. "The air in Denver is good enough," she said. "Besides, I don't want to change anything anymore."

Her words, so softly yet so deliberately spoken, weighed him down as if they were iron.

"I'm sorry to hear that, Lilly." And he truly was, but at the same time he was glad he'd found her again. Glad and frightened, both.

She slid off the bed and moved effortlessly toward him and knelt at his knees. Her scent was powerful now, as it had been the other times when he'd been with her. He threw the drink down his throat, hoping it would calm him, but it did not; even with the additional fortification, his hands shook as he reached out to touch her hair. He held back a little, as if she would burn his fingertips, and an involuntary sigh escaped from him before he could stop it.

She laughed again, and the hardness of it made his blood run cold, but then she looked up at him as frankly as always, and her eyes were liquid and shining and not at all cruel. "There's really nothing I want to change, Arnold," she said. "Nothing." She was intense, serious, telling him this thing earnestly and utterly without guile.

Then, in the way her pupils contracted, in the particular shining of her eyes, he saw that her old demon still held her in its sway.

Which explained everything.

"You're still smoking opium," he said simply.

A trace of a smile played across her lips, and her eyes closed slowly, then opened. "It helps me live," she said. "I don't use it very often. Not since I came here." The lie was utterly transparent to him even through the alcoholic haze; she'd smoked opium within the hour. Her weakness reminded him of his own, and it shamed him.

"I helps me to live," she said again, as if no other explanation were needed.

He extended his hand in spite of his unfathomable fear of her and stroked her hair gently. It seemed odd somehow that she should be so warm; her skin was the color and texture of alabaster, and he half expected her to be as cold as hewn stone. He'd seen her too many times when she'd been cold as death, with the power of the narcotic drawing her into such a deep sleep it had been impossible to awaken her.

As his fingertips danced lightly over the thin line of the part in her hair, he took a deep breath to shake off the effects of the liquor, if only for a few moments. He tried an old trick to see if it would help: it was likely to be a useless exercise, but even so, he had to try to catalog everything in her room, try as in the old days to commit everything to memory, if only to draw his mind away from the terrible temptation at his feet. Once, when he was the best lawman between Kansas and California, he would have been able to lock a picture of the room into his memory for recall at any moment, but of course the rye whiskey had destroyed that skill, among so many others.

He ignored the buzzing in his brain and concentrated every bit of his energy on the task.

Unlike an ordinary whore's crib, her room was cluttered with many possessions, some of them little more than knickknacks he vaguely recalled having seen before. Some were expensive, probably gifts from gentleman callers: the pearl necklace or ostrich-feather boa or ornate silver bluestone brooch on her dressing table. Other items were like bits and pieces from a child's room, jarringly out of place: a cornshuck doll, a little girl's broken teacup, a tattered bit of a child's quilt.

His hands shook and he wanted another drink. He couldn't be angry with her, even though he knew he should: there was no point in chastising her for her weakness, when he was so ready to succumb to his own.

"Does your father know you're here?" he asked after a time.

The effect on her was instantaneous. She pulled away as if he'd slapped her and glared at him with genuine anger.

"Well, does he?"

"Don't talk about him," she said. "Please don't." Then her sudden fury faded, and she looked up at him with wide, soft eyes. The change from anger to serenity was so complete it was as if she'd slipped on a mask, and whether it was acting or opium or both, it fit the true Lilly Morgan well.

As it always had.

He took another deep breath. "Are they treating you well?" he asked.

"Yes," she said, and she moved toward him again and brushed her long white fingers along his knee. "They are very kind to me here."

"I'm glad."

"You're trembling, Arnold. Do you want a drink?"

He licked his lips with his thickened tongue. "I'm all right."

"There's a whole bottle here."

He wiped his mouth with the back of his hand. "I'm fine," he said, struggling successfully against his own addiction for the moment.

She rose to her feet and stood before him, her movements fluid and effortless and precise. Her satin-covered navel was just at eye level.

"Do you want to make love, or do you want to talk tonight?" she asked so quietly he scarcely heard her.

He wondered how many times before she had asked that question of him and countless others. But with him, at least, the answer had always been the same.

"Talk," he mumbled. "Just talk."

"Arnold, it's time to go," Alvarez said as patiently as he could.

Toothacker looked up at him from the cot and then down at his bloody hands again. No, not yet. Not before he had sorted through this business one more time.

Lilly Morgan was remarkable. There was absolutely no doubt about that. She had an amazing gift in being able to draw him out of himself so completely that the pain of the years fell away, leaving him strong and whole, as if he were twenty again. And she did it with such little effort. If it was acting, it was nonetheless wonderful. Perhaps that was why he loved her beyond measure or reason. He knew for certain that was why he'd never made love to her. Beyond his unwillingness to violate the oath of fidelity he'd taken so long ago when he'd married, Toothacker believed having sex with Lilly Morgan would surely spoil the astounding bond of friendship that—in his heart at least—had existed between them since their very first evenings together. No other woman had ever been able to make him feel so loving and alive, not even Gertrude in the best of their early days together.

And especially not Gertrude in recent years, when her own strength seemed to mock his weakness at every turn.

Toothacker had known Lilly Morgan always, it seemed—certainly since she was in grammar school, when she was nothing more than the daughter of an important acquaintance. Yet even then, he'd been drawn to this marvelous, fascinating, sad child. He'd watched her through the years as her stern banker father tried to mold her to his will by beating the life and spirit out of her. Perhaps Jacob Morgan was only trying to do what was best for a headstrong girl (or so Gertrude always said), but the results were tragic. Toothacker and the rest of Pueblo watched her turn temperamental and then rebellious at the laying on of the strap and fist, and they watched her drift into associations with the wrong people and ultimately into prostitution as a way of getting back at her father.

Only after old Jacob had lost her completely to one of Pueblo's least respectable madams did he seek the counsel of his friends, and it was Arnold Toothacker who agreed to try to talk some sense into the girl.

It was to his everlasting shame that he'd botched the rescue so completely.

At Jacob Morgan's bidding, he began visiting the bawdy house where the girl lived, always asking only for her. With Morgan paying for the time, Arnold was supposed to find a way to convince her to return home. But his long talks with her, his feeble attempts at monopolizing her time so she wouldn't be able to be with other men, had a most unexpected outcome. She was a remarkably observant young woman with an instinctive ability to read her customers' needs, and it didn't take long for her to uncover a deep vein of unhappiness in her putative rescuer; within weeks, he was visiting her on his own, spending his own money to be with her. And always just to talk.

It was around that time that someone, perhaps the madam or one of her gentleman callers—it hardly mattered who—introduced her to opium. Lilly lost herself in the pipe almost at once; her energy waned and her weight dropped alarmingly. Arnold was slow to recognize the signs—in large measure, he had to admit, because of his own weakness for the bottle—and so it was already too late by the time he came to his senses and tried to talk her out of the habit. It was a pointless exercise, anyway. The narcotic trances distanced her from everything around her. Conversations with her became one-sided affairs barely more satisfying than talking to a statue, and after several months of trying, he stopped seeing her.

Within a few months there were rumors that she'd drifted from town to a whorehouse up in the mining camps, then that she'd died of the poison effects of the opium.

There was hell to pay with old Jacob Morgan, and Toothacker found himself ostracized by old friends and acquainttances. Gertrude, as usual, was a pillar of strength, which didn't help at all. Only the bottle eased the pain.

Then one night, almost a year later, he ran into her father on the street, and rather than giving him a tongue-lashing, the old man was aglow with happiness. He said that Lilly had given up opium and come home on her own—no thanks to Arnold Toothacker—and was soon to leave for San Francisco to live with an uncle, where she would begin a career working as a governess for another banker.

Toothacker saw her twice after that, both times in the company of her father, and both times at a distance. It broke his heart to see her without being able to talk to her as he had in her whore's crib.

And now she was here, just inches away.

"You should have gone to San Francisco," he said, his voice cracking. He poured himself another rye, spilling a little, but he didn't drink it. He owed her that much.

She ran her fingers through his thinning hair and pressed her body against his shoulder, pulling his head into her stomach. She was warm, and the incredible intoxicating smell of her engulfed him. In spite of the rye, he felt the ancient stirrings in his manhood; shame and embarrassment and excitement and pride all threatened to consume him at once. He pushed her away and tossed down his drink. He drank and poured and drank again, this time spilling most of it.

She slipped away from him and drifted across the room to the edge of her bed.

"Arnold, come to me. No talking tonight. Please." Her voice was thin and brittle and completely seductive. He couldn't refuse her, nor did he dare succumb to her.

She beckoned again and stretched out on the bed, white skin on white satin. He stood cautiously, managing to take a few steps before the room swam around him. He grabbed at the canopy above her bed and steadied himself, then took a deep breath and held it until the room stopped spinning. Suddenly, anger welled up in him and it was deep and real—anger at himself for the weakling he was and at her for the shallow seductress she had allowed herself to become.

"Arnold, please." She pulled the gown up around her exquisite thighs, exposing supple white flesh, and opened her legs to him.

"No," he said without conviction. It was a struggle to get out the single word. "No."

He must not. Must never.

And then it all started to move. The room began to re-volve slowly, tilting over on its side.

He gripped the canopy tighter to steady himself, but it was no use; the room heaved wildly, and all he could do was close his eyes against it.

He heard her voice, as if from across the void, and he forced his eyes open. He looked down at her.

She was stretched out on the bed, white and cold-looking and still as marble, incredibly young and beautiful. But something was different, something he couldn't quite figure out.

"Lay here with me, Arnold," she said. "You'll feel better." She reached out to him, held something up to him. "Here. Try this."

It was her pipe. The demon opium.

He tried to say something, but only made some sound

even he didn't recognize and slapped at the evil thing, knocking it out of her hand. It crashed into something across the room. He turned to see what he'd done, but she was already out of the bed, going for the pipe, moving in what seemed like slow motion, yet she was far quicker than he.

Toothacker raised his hand again to strike her, to keep her from the opium. For her sake. For his own sake. And for more than that. Terrible rage boiled over in him and snatched a grotesque snarl from his throat.

But then the room whirled again and he couldn't stop it, and he slipped away from himself into oblivion.

Alvarez stretched his bad leg and stifled a yawn. He still had a nagging headache behind his right eye, and he was damn tired of waiting on a weepy old alcoholic.

"Arnold, come on," he demanded. "The police aren't going to charge you for a while. As a favor to you. And to me."

Toothacker looked up, his eyes blank. "Is she dead?"

Alvarez nodded.

Toothacker shook his head. "I don't remember what happened. I was there with her, and then I passed out, I suppose. When I woke up, there was blood everywhere. And she..." His voice trailed off. "She looked so cold."

Alvarez cleared his throat. Toothacker was such a pitiful sight it embarrassed him. "Well, they're not charging you until they look into it a little further. But you have to stay put with either me or Ben Comstock." He shifted his weight off his bad leg and cleared his throat again. Protective custody: that was what Ted Paine had called it, but what it really meant was that he and Ben would be responsible for

Arnold—held accountable if he tried anything stupid.

Alvarez cleared his throat again impatiently. "The commissioner is going to bend the rules a little for you because of everything you did in the old days. For services rendered, you might say."

Toothacker rose slowly and shuffled over to the barred door. His hands were trembling as if palsied.

"You ready?" Alvarez asked gruffly.

Toothacker nodded.

"He's ready," Alvarez called over his shoulder to the guard.

"She looked so cold," Toothacker said again to no one in particular.

Police Commissioner Theodore Paine arranged the papers into a neat pike and signed the top one, then laid his pen down and leaned back in his big leather-covered chair and took a deep drag on the black Cuban cigar he'd lit moments before. He considered the two men seated before him through the smoke haze. The big humidor filled with cigars stood open in the center of the ornate mahogany desk; he pointed toward it.

"Please, Tom, have a cigar. They're the finest smokes in Denver. Maybe the finest west of Chicago. I pride myself on always having plenty of fresh cigars."

Alvarez smiled his thanks and took a cigar, sniffed at it appreciatively, and slipped it into a coat pocket. The cigar had the nutty-sweet aroma of expensive tobaccos, and the humidor had kept it perfectly: supple, soft to the touch, but not damp. Being the commissioner of police must pay handsomely in Denver, Alvarez thought idly; an inspector at the federal prison in Leavenworth would never have been able to afford Cuban cigars and mahogany office furniture.

Paine blew out another cloud of smoke and turned his frank gaze on his other guest. "You're free to go now, Arnold," he said with clipped, professional pleasantry. "Just stay where we can find you in case we need to question you further."

"I'd... like to help you find her killer," Toothacker mumbled, brushing the back of his hand absently across the stains on his clothing. In a room filled with the civilized odors of leather and polished furniture and good cigars, he stank of whiskey and vomit and especially the sweet-salty odor of blood. "I didn't kill the girl. I hope you know that."

Paine sniffed and straightened the papers and took a drag on the cigar again. "I'm sure you didn't, but you have to understand how it looks. Her skull was crushed and she'd been stabbed in the throat repeatedly. We found you in her room with her blood all over you, and by your own admission, you've known her for some time."

Toothacker's eyes darted past Paine's face and then into his lap again. "Did you find the weapon?"

"On the floor, not five feet from her body." Paine glanced at Alvarez, who'd already seen the carved stone figurine the killer had used to bash in the girl's head.

"But I didn't kill her," Toothacker said softly. "Not her."

"No, I'm sure not," Paine said with a perfunctory detachment that told both Alvarez and Toothacker he didn't mean it. He rose and thrust his hands into his trouser pockets. It was an act of dismissal. "I'd like to speak to you alone before you go, Tom."

Toothacker rose unsteadily. "I want to help you find the killer," he said without making eye contact with the commissioner.

"That won't be necessary," Paine said icily.

"But I want to. Let me see her room, at least. Maybe seeing it again will help me remember something… useful."

Paine waved it off. "Perhaps you don't understand, Marshal. You're a suspect in the woman's murder. I'm sticking my neck out just letting you out of jail. The only place you're going is back to the hotel with Tom."

Toothacker picked at some dried blood on his trousers. "I want to help."

"Then stay the hell out of the way. Understand?" Paine walked around his desk and steered Toothacker out the door and into the arms of a waiting guard, then stepped back into the office and closed the door.

"I know he's one of Colorado's most respected citizens. Or at least he was," he said. "Now he's just a common sot. I'll wager he was too damn drunk to know what he was doing when he killed that girl, but still and all, I have to believe he did kill her."

Alvarez sighed. In spite of Arnold's faults, he didn't want to believe it, but the facts seemed plain enough. "You'll continue your investigation, though?" he asked, hoping it didn't sound too judgmental, one way or the other.

Paine gave him a cold little smile. "Of course I will. That's my job."

"Sorry, I didn't mean anything."

"I don't want to see this hung on someone with a past as honorable as his any more than you do, especially since the woman in question was a common whore. Ordinarily, the death of one of these women wouldn't create much stir. Some men in my position might even be tempted to ignore it altogether. The trouble is, the Corcoran woman is, shall we say, well connected? Very well connected politically." He gave Alvarez a knowing look that froze the smile in place. "So we couldn't keep this a secret if we wanted to."

"Of course," Alvarez agreed, but he thought he saw something fleeting in the commissioner's eyes, something that had been triggered by the mention of politics. In Alvarez's experience, good lawmen avoided politics like the plague. But then, Paine was city police; they were a different breed, and these were different times. After a moment's hesitation, he let it go. He was tired and his head hurt; all he really wanted to do was go back to the hotel and sleep.

"If there's another explanation, we'll find it," Paine said. "You can be sure of that. Just keep a close eye on him, Tom. That's important. If there's anything you need, don't hesitate to let me know. And for God's sake, don't let him go back to the house."

Alvarez nodded. "We'll look after him, Ted." He offered his hand, and Paine shook it.

"I appreciate it," Paine said as Alvarez took his leave. "I surely do."

Both men were completely aware that at that very moment the responsibility for Arnold Toothacker formally and officially passed from the Denver Police Department to two retired peace officers, and the commissioner of police didn't try to hide his relief. He took a self-satisfied puff on the cigar and blew the smoke out in a slow stream that drifted toward the ceiling.

Chapter 7

THE SEPTEMBER WEATHER WAS SHOWING SIGNS of taking a decided turn for the worse. Since dawn, slate gray clouds had been gathering around the granite ramparts west of the city, obscuring the peaks, and a north wind scudding down the front range had the sting of impending winter to it.

Alvarez pulled up his coat collar against the chill while he and Toothacker walked the six blocks from the police station to the hotel. Passersby pretended not to notice Toothacker's bloodstained attire, stumbling gait, and forlorn look, but they gave them a wide berth just the same.

"You have a spare suit at the hotel?" Alvarez asked after they'd gone several blocks.

Toothacker said he did.

Alvarez hunkered down in the warmth of his coat. "We'll have the hotel draw you a bath and get you into clean clothes. You'll feel better then," he said.

Toothacker reached out a trembling hand and took Alvarez's arm. "I didn't kill her. Bill Cody took me there. I didn't even know she was in Denver. It was pure accident that I found her. We talked, and I must have passed out. I had a lot to drink last night, but I didn't kill her. As God is my judge."

Alvarez pried Toothacker's fingers off his sleeve. "Then you don't have anything to worry about, do you? Ted Paine's boys will find the killer and you'll be off the hook and that will be that."

"You don't believe me, do you?"

Alvarez didn't answer.

"What happened to Cody?" Toothacker asked after they'd walked in silence for another block.

Alvarez stopped to blow his nose. What the hell, he thought. Why not tell him? "Paine says they found him in the madam's room when they went to question her. Somehow our gallant old Bill had lost his trousers and couldn't find them anywhere. No pants, but he still had that fancy shirt on, and those ridiculous thigh-high riding boots. How the hell you can lose your pants and not your boots is beyond me." The whole business left a bad taste in his mouth.

Toothacker shrugged, not caring at all about Buffalo Bill's predicament. "But he hadn't heard anything?"

"No one did. Some hunchback—what did Paine say his name was?—he found you."

Toothacker struggled to come up with the name. "Ulysses."

"That's the one. Ulysses. He found you and the woman, both lying in a pool of blood. Said he was just checking to see whether you needed anything, and found her. She was dead, of course."

Toothacker shook his head sadly. "I know there was

blood everywhere. I remember that. I just don't remember what happened." A woman walking toward them caught sight of Toothacker and quickly raised a dainty handkerchief to her face as if to ward off some foul odor, but Toothacker seemed not to notice. "Her father hired me to turn her away from that life, you know, and so all I ever did was talk to her. Last night, I was standing there, just talking, and then I must have passed out. The next thing I knew I was sitting at the foot of her bed and she was dead on the floor beside me. The police had come already, I think, but I'm not sure. But I know I didn't kill her. As God is my judge."

The spattering of cold drizzle began to fall from the leaden skies, and Alvarez, saying nothing, leaned into the wind and marched up the street, leaving Toothacker to follow.

Comstock was waiting for them in the Drover's lobby. He pulled Alvarez aside.

"Weather's turning nasty, I see," he said.

"To hell with the weather. What are we going to do with this old bastard?"

Comstock rolled his eyes. "Damn good question. Look, Tom, I've juggled the accommodations," he said, and nodded in the direction of the desk clerk, who was doing his best to make it look like he wasn't eavesdropping. "Or should I say the local constables did. They moved me and him into the room next door to yours." He didn't sound happy about it. "How the hell did I get mixed up in this?"

"You shouldn't be surprised. You made such a fine impression on Commissioner Paine last night."

Comstock grimaced. "I suppose." He waved Toothacker over. "Arnold, I've moved your things in with me."

"Why?" He wiped the stained sleeve of his coat across his cracked lips.

Alvarez answered for both of them. "Because you're under arrest, dammit. Haven't you figured that out yet? We're your jailers. Now don't you think it's time you tried to get in touch with your wife, so she knows what kind of trouble you're in?"

Toothacker's eyes opened wide, and the muscles in his jaw worked for a long time before any sound came out. "I don't think so. Not yet. Besides, I didn't do it. Just let me go back to Mrs. Corcoran's and I can prove it. Please, Thomas."

"Over my dead body."

"Please. I know I can help find the killer. I used to be the best tracker in Colorado."

"To be honest, Arnold, I'm not sure you could track your way out of this hotel right now," Alvarez snapped. "Now if you don't mind, Ben, he's all yours. I'm going to get some sleep." Then he turned his back on them and headed up to his room.

The drone of voices in the ballroom buzzed around him as Tom Alvarez sipped at the mock turtle soup without tasting it. His mind was a thousand miles away. A few hours of sleep hadn't done a thing for his lingering hangover; with every heartbeat he felt the pulsing pain behind his eye. And to add insult to injury, this second night of conventioneering was even worse than the first. The usual round of drinks before dinner had been almost more than he could bear, with the same bunch of old boys telling the same old lies over and over again; the cocktail-hour entertainment had been a college glee club intent on showing off youthful enthusiasm in front of a bunch of old men while a photographer burned up copious quantities of flash power taking everyone's picture.

The only saving grace was that Alvarez was shed of Arnold Toothacker, at least for the time being. Comstock had lost the toss to see who got to play jailer in their rooms until the temptations of the cocktail hour had passed and dinner had been served, which seemed only simple justice to Alvarez under the circumstances; after all, Ben hadn't been the one who had to suffer the indignity of fetching the old reprobate from the police station.

Still, as Alvarez sipped at the soup, he couldn't escape the nagging thought he'd awakened with. As a lawman, Arnold had been a thinker, not a fighter; he'd brought in more live prisoners than most frontier marshals, and he'd even been known to testify for some of them if he thought they were getting a raw deal. He'd always been cool in tough scrapes, the last man to draw his weapon or fire a shot. He'd been a man of high principles in unprincipled times, and Alvarez had admired him mightily in those days.

Alvarez pushed his soup away and consulted the fancy printed program.

The evening's after-dinner speaker was a pinch-faced little inspector on the Denver force whose topic was the latest in scientific police procedures. Alvarez had overheard him talking with Tilghman, Masterson, and Earp before dinner about the newest techniques, and Alvarez couldn't decide whether he found the little man's condescending tone and highfalutin language or Earp's fawning the more irritating.

He wished he were shed of this whole business.

The blood-rare steaks and boiled potatoes came. Alvarez poked at the underdone meat and ate the rest slowly, expecting Comstock and his prisoner to show up at any moment; by the time the coffee and little pieces of spongecake were served, he'd decided he better go looking.

He didn't have to go far.

Comstock was already in the lobby with two coats draped over his arms—his own and Alvarez's—and he gave Alvarez a sheepish grin as soon as he saw him.

"He slipped out," Comstock said so softly it came out a whisper.

Alvarez sighed. "Christ almighty, Ben. How the hell did you let him…"

Comstock shrugged. "I know. I know. He had to use the toilet, and I let him go by himself." He held Alvarez's coat out to him. "At least he'll be easy to find on a night like this. All he had on was a shirt and trousers. Besides, I think I know where he'll go."

Alvarez massaged his temples. "That doesn't take a damn genius. He'll go to that damn whorehouse." He took his coat and slipped it on.

Comstock nodded. "He talked some more about the girl, Tom. I don't think he killed her."

They headed out the wide front door of the Drovers and let the doorman hail them a hansom.

"My hunch is that you've gone soft in your old age, letting him get away from you," Alvarez said.

"Well, if you ask me, maybe we owe it to him to help him prove his innocence. For old time's sake, you might say."

"You're only saying that because you let him get away," Alvarez said gruffly. He reached into his vest pocket for the cigar Ted Paine had given him. The smoke would be good in the cold wetness of a September night. In spite of the headache and the company. And the errand.

He thought idly of his old Smith and Wesson in the bureau drawer.

Chapter 8

Toothacker beat them to Margaret Corcoran's place, but the hunchback Ulysses had thrown him out into the yard, and that's where Alvarez and Comstock found him, shivering and nursing bruised ribs. So long as they were there, they ought to do something, Comstock said, and Alvarez reluctantly relented. They decided to use the oldest and simplest plan for lawmen working as a team: divide and conquer. Comstock took Toothacker with him upstairs to interrogate the Madam while Alvarez interviewed the hunchback. Later they'd compare notes and dig into any discrepancies they discovered. If there were any discrepancies.

Alvarez leaned back on Margaret Corcoran's red velvet settee and took a last long drag on his cigar, then dropped the stub into a gleaming brass spittoon. The pungent smoke helped mask the sweet female odors of French perfume, talcum powder, and rosewater soap crowding in on him. The girls were nowhere to be found, having been sent off to their cribs early by the Madam, but their stink was everywhere.

Alvarez had never been one to frequent cathouses, and they always made him nervous. Not because he was a prude, but because he felt that the women in these places were so inferior to the sort of women he admired that he wanted nothing whatever to do with them under any circumstances. To his way of thinking, these weak-willed creatures scarcely deserved to be called women. When he thought of his wife or his dearly departed mother or the hundreds of other pioneer women he'd known through the years, what came to mind was their toughness and tenderness, their ability to do hard physical work alongside their men, the fierce way they protected and nurtured their children, their determination and inner strength, their resolve to face the hardships of life head-on no matter the cost. Those women were the equal—and sometimes the better—of any man.

In the old days, when women were few in the frontier settlements, many of the saloon-hall girls had been sturdy stock, working hard for a stake or looking hard for a decent man who could take them out of their cribs. But in Alvarez's mind, these modern whores weren't like that at all. Or not many of them were, anyway. In his experience, the big-city, high-tone whores like Mrs. Corcoran's were silly, emotional creatures with little physical stamina and less moral fiber. Their contemporary small-town sisters were just as likely to be pathetic creatures, plain-looking and overworked farm girls with no money and no prospects. Either way, they seemed fit only for a life of shame and degradation while they waited for disease or fatigue to relieve them of their earthly burdens. He felt sorry for the whores, but was repelled by them at the same time; for the life of him, he couldn't understand why other men felt the need of such women. A tip of his hat to a respectable wo-man walking down a dusty Wichita street gave Tom Alvarez a deeper measure of human companionship than he could imagine getting from a night of rutting with some soft, sweet-scented, mindless girl wasting her life away in a whore's crib. To Alvarez's way of thinking, the fact that other men did, in fact, need to spend time with whores said as much about the lamentable weakness in the male animal as it did about the fallen women. Maybe more.

He sighed and tried to shift his mind away from such pointless meanderings and toward the business at hand—business he was sure they'd be better off leaving to Ted Paine and the Denver Police.

He heard a thumping noise from upstairs. Probably the Madam's stout cane pounding the floor as she listened to Comstock's impertinent questions. In spite of himself, Alvarez smiled to think of Ben pacing back and forth, getting the woman's side of the story in the room where Bill Cody had lost his trousers.

Too bad he'd missed seeing the Great Scout of the Plains standing there in his fancy shirt and those ridiculous thigh boots and no pants.

Always a showman, that Cody.

He felt some better just thinking about it.

The heavy beechwood door swung open and the hunchback stumped into the room. Alvarez stood to greet him, but neither man offered a hand.

The hunchback had a broad, expressionless, handsome face with a yellowed complexion that made him look like a mulatto or perhaps vaguely Oriental. His jet black eyes focused on Alvarez's and didn't waver when he settled himself into an overstuffed chair near the settee. In spite of his twisted spine, his hand-tailored woolen suit and crisp white shirt fit impeccably. He sank into the cushions, leaving his chin scant inches from his knees and his feet dangling a few inches off the floor, but there was nothing comical or self-pitying about him. Alvarez knew instinctively the man was dangerous.

"Good evening to you, sir," Ulysses said after a moment, his tone heavy with sarcasm.

"The house is very quiet this evening," Alvarez said as pleasantly as he could. "Why so?" He already knew the answer, as was his custom in interrogations, but he waited for the man to tell him just the same.

"We have decided it would be best for business to remain closed until after the funeral, sir." Ulysses sniffed, his black eyes still locked onto Alvarez's.

Alvarez nodded knowingly. "The police shut you down."

Ulysses tilted his head ever so slightly. "There was a suggestion that it would be unseemly to remain open for business, and we concurred. The gentlemen who frequent Madam's would refrain from dropping by out of respect for the departed in any case." Ulysses smiled, showing his small, pointed teeth. His soft Southern accent was oddly out of place with the formal diction.

"Of course." Alvarez straightened up a little. "Now, if you'd be so kind as to give me your full name, please."

The hunchback's gaze hardened. "Ulysses."

"Ulysses what?"

"Just Ulysses." The smile widened into an insult and a challenge.

"I assume you have a last name?"

"I do, but I've had no need of it in years. I am known

throughout the region as Ulysses, and that will do you well enough for now, Marshal."

Alvarez decided not to press the point, at least not for now. "Tell me about last night. About the killing."

"There's nothing to tell."

"Tell me what you do know."

The black eyes closed for a moment and then re-opened. "I took your friend Toothacker to the girl's room at the behest of Madam and Colonel Cody. I brought him a bottle of very good rye whiskey, which he drank like water. When I stopped by the room some time later to see whether anything more was needed, the girl was dead. Mr. Tooth-acker was standing over her body."

"That's all?"

"That's all," Ulysses said, showing the teeth again.

Alvarez nodded. Unless he missed his guess, he'd just heard word-for-word what Ulysses had told Ted Paine's men. "What time did you take him to the room? What time did you find the girl dead?"

"I'm not entirely certain. We were quite busy last night."

"Guess," Alvarez said, letting his growing impatience show.

"Midnight. Midnight to two. Something like that."

"You took him to the room at midnight and discovered the body at two?"

Ulysses nodded.

"What did you know about the girl?"

"Nothing. She came to us several weeks ago and Madam granted her the back room."

"Did she have any regular customers? Or enemies you know of?"

Ulysses ran his tongue over his pointed teeth before answering. "We are very discreet here, Mr. Alvarez. I would not tell you even if I knew."

"Do you know?"

Ulysses smiled.

Alvarez stared back, waiting.

Ulysses held the frozen smile.

Alvarez arched an eyebrow and focused his gaze on the very center of Ulysses' black eyes. The pupils contracted, then dilated again. He felt like laughing. It was a simple game, a contest of wills—and whoever moved or spoke first would lose. This was just like the old days. God, he'd forgotten how much he loved it!

Ben Comstock paced the length of the ornate, brocade-curtained, garishly papered room and turned and paced back, moving slowly. Eight paces. Twenty feet—a big room. He hoped this deliberate measuring of each step was having the desired effect on Mrs. Corcoran, but he couldn't be sure. The woman, who sat watching him from her perch on a throne-like Chippendale chair at the foot of her huge bed, was a good actress and as iron-willed as most successful women of her kind. Only Arnold Toothacker seemed bothered by the pacing. Wrapped in a heavy blanket, he sat uncomfortably on the edge of the bed, clutching a glass of sherry in both hands.

"You really should sip the wine, my dear Mr. Toothacker," the woman said evenly without taking her eyes from Ben Comstock. "It will warm you."

Comstock decided she would have been handsome once, before age had added flesh to her face and neck. But she'd covered the sagging skin with powder and rouge for so many years she looked gray and naked without it now.

He stopped pacing abruptly. "Tell me again what you knew about the girl."

Margaret Corcoran cleared her throat delicately. "She came highly recommended from an acquaintance of mine in Pueblo. She was an intelligent girl. A very good conversationalist."

For a moment, Toothacker's attention shifted from the sherry to the woman.

"What else?" Comstock asked.

"That's all."

"All?"

The woman let her irritation show by taking a deep breath and letting it out noisily. "Mr. Comstock," she said, "one learns certain discretions in a business such as mine. Certain things are not asked if they are not important to the business at hand. The girl was clean and intelligent and came highly recommended. I had no need to know anything further."

"And she was no trouble to you while she stayed here?"

"Not until last night."

"Do you think Marshal Toothacker here killed her?"

The woman turned her steady gaze on Toothacker, then dismissed him as if he were a gnat. "No one else had access to her room," she said evenly. "I find it hard to believe that he did not kill her."

Toothacker seemed more interested in the wine than her answer. After a moment, he lifted the glass to his lips and drank it down.

"Your man had access," Comstock said evenly.

She swung her heavy head around and her eyes, narrowed to slits, met his, but Comstock noted that the gray features bore no red stain of anger. She was acting again, but not well enough. She'd expected this charge, which meant she'd thought of it herself. Still, she was a worthy opponent in this little bull-baiting game.

"Ulysses is completely trustworthy," she said.

"How do you know?"

"We have been together for many years. I would trust him with my life. More than that, I would trust him with the future of my business. I needn't tell you a killing like this takes a serious toll on *that*." She gave him a quick smile that was as brittle and false as a plaster-of-paris mask.

Comstock began pacing again. "Did she have any enemies that you know of? Enemies from Pueblo?"

"None."

"You're sure?"

The woman took in another deep breath. "Don't you think I'd have rejected her out of hand if she had known enemies? A woman in my position has far too much to lose by taking in trash. The girl was *not* trash."

Comstock took a few paces and changed tactics. "Tell me what you heard last night. After Arnold went to the girl's room."

"Nothing."

He deliberately turned his back to her. "Nothing? In a house filled with fornicators?" Then he spun around quickly to see her reaction. "You heard nothing?"

The plaster smile cracked at the edges. "I run a civilized establishment. No one is permitted to get boisterous. We insist on maintaining the necessary civilities at all times."

"How about later, when you retired to your room with Colonel Cody? Did you hear anything then? Or just the rustling of your own petticoats?"

Her eyes blazed with sudden fury, but she brought her temper under control in an instant. "I told you I heard nothing, Mr. Comstock," she said, with such forced sweetness that Toothacker looked up from the empty glass in his hands. "And I will say nothing about Colonel Cody, so save your breath. He is an old friend. He gave his statement to the police."

Comstock gave her a lascivious leer. "Buffalo Bill is a friend of mine, too," he said, enjoying the lie. "We go back a long way together. I sure as hell don't want to tarnish old Bill's sterling reputation. I just want to help my friend here. He says he's innocent, and—"

"I have to see her room," Toothacker interrupted. "I have to." He rose from his seat on the bed and swayed unsteadily. He looked incredibly old and tired. He took a deep breath to strengthen his resolve. "I will see her room!"

Mrs. Corcoran pushed herself off her throne. "Absolutely not!"

Toothacker eyed the empty sherry glass sadly and tossed it onto the bed. "I have to," he said again, his voice cracking, and he started to weep.

She laughed. It was a cold, calculating laugh meant to increase his shame. "You shan't go traipsing through this house alarming my other girls!" the woman snapped, and she thumped her cane on the floor for emphasis. "It's bad enough that I've let the lot of you in at all! I run a quality house here."

Toothacker wiped at his cheeks with the sleeve of his coat. "I didn't kill her, Mrs. Corcoran. I just have to see the room, that's all." He took a deep breath. "Not what I'm sober."

The woman thumped the cane again, but Toothacker

was already heading for the open door and the staircase at the end of the hall.

"Damn you!" she called, then waddled after him without waiting for Ben Comstock.

The woman's screaming and swearing brought Alvarez and the hunchback on the run. Toothacker was already in the girl's room, but she ordered the hunchback to fetch the police, and before either Comstock or Alvarez could stop him, Ulysses had muscled his way past them and bolted out the front door, leaving them little to do but wait for Toothacker to finish looking around. Alvarez kept watch while Comstock prodded the old alcoholic on. Once Ulysses got back with the police, they'd all be carted off for sure. At best, they had only a few minutes before they'd have to leave—or face certain arrest for trespass.

The girl's room was a disaster. The police had turned it inside out, and they hadn't taken the trouble to straighten up when they finished. Her belongings were laid out on the bloodstained bedspread, where someone had been tagging and cataloging them, and the delicate lace of the canopy had been torn down. The blood on the floor had dried black and crusty where no one had bothered yet to clean it up. Comstock stood in the doorway, blocking Mrs. Corcoran from interfering while Toothacker rocked on his heels and stared down at the bed.

"I'll see you swing for killing that girl!" the woman hissed from the hallway as she pressed a perfumed silk handkerchief to her nose to keep out the smell of death and decay.

Toothacker ignored the warning. He moved slowly around the bed, allowing his eyes to roam over everything once, twice, three times.

"I don't know," he said aloud. "I just don't know." He closed his eyes and tried to *feel* the room the way it should have been, the way he'd seen it the night before. He knew her spirit was there, and he wanted to feel its presence—as he might have in the old days, when his friends the last of the Arapaho buffalo hunters had taught him how to sense the earth spirit in everything, from the ripe July grass to the great bison herds to the cold, noisy streams overflowing with mountain snowmelt. Now those free hunters were reduced to sad old white-haired men imprisoned in square wooden houses in Oklahoma rather than on their old hunting grounds, but the great truth of their medicine was still strong.

And might, for a moment, make Toothacker strong as well. All he needed was time. He stretched himself out, held his breath, kept his eyes shut tight, *felt*.

Nothing.

He slumped against the bed frame and let his breath out with a sigh.

A clock somewhere deep in the bowels of the house struck eleven.

"This is crazy, Ben. Let's get going," Alvarez urged from the hallway. "That man's been gone twenty minutes already."

"He's right, Arnold. Let's go," Comstock agreed.

Toothacker's eyes fluttered open. He made another complete turn in an attempt to take it all in, but Comstock caught his arm and pulled him into the hallway.

"I'm telling the police you were here," Mrs. Corcoran screeched, raising her cane as she followed them down the hall and driving them like cattle. "It's my civic duty to tell them you're abroad with a murderer."

Alvarez reached the heavy front door first and pulled it open. A gust of cold, dry wind whipped through the doorway. "Damn Denver weather," he muttered to no one in particular. "Let's get this old drunk back to the hotel before he catches his death."

The woman swung her cane at them, nearly losing her balance as the last shreds of patience abandoned her.

"Good idea," Comstock said as he struggled to get Toothacker across the threshold.

"Something was missing," Arnold said, turning on the woman. "She had a brooch. A bluestone brooch. On her bureau. It wasn't with the other things on her bed."

Mrs. Corcoran started to take another swipe at him with the cane, but she stopped dead still in mid-swing. "I don't know any bluestone brooch," she said warily.

"Come on Arnold." Comstock pulled on his arm.

"Tell them, please, about the missing brooch," Toothacker pleaded. "It was on her bureau and now it's gone."

"There's no brooch," the woman said, and she poked him again, sending him through the doorway and onto the porch. "Jail's the place for you. Now begone! You'll not be welcome in my establishment again!"

"Tell them about the brooch!" Toothacker shouted back at her over his shoulder as Comstock and Alvarez hustled him off the porch and across the yard.

She slammed the heavy door in answer.

Behind her, down the long hallway, a door that had been open a few inches closed silently, except for the metal-on-metal click of a deadbolt sliding into place, but Margaret Corcoran failed to notice it. She was lost in thought for a moment, then she shrugged and stumped off to her parlor to await the police.

Chapter 9

SOMEONE RAPPED SHARPLY THREE TIMES ON THE DOOR. Tom Alvarez came grudgingly awake before the third rap, pulling himself up out of the black bottomless pit of dreamless sleep. He threw off the blanket and sat up on the edge of the bed. It was still black night; he reached out for the old alarm clock in its familiar place, but it wasn't there.

Of course it wasn't. This was Denver, and a hotel room.

The room was cold, too cold for an old man in his long johns.

Whoever was at the door knocked again.

"Hold your horses, dammit!" Alvarez barked.

He groped around for the tattered old robe at the foot of the bed, pulled it on, and padded across the room. He couldn't remember exactly where the lamp was, but a thin strip of yellow light shining under the door showed him what he had to aim for. Even so, he stubbed his toe on the claw foot of an unseen and unremembered chair, swore, and pushed the door open.

The pimply-faced bellboy, his hand raised to knock again, took an automatic step backward to keep out of harm's way.

"What the hell do you want?"

The boy gave Alvarez a sheepish grin. He stuttered, and had to close his eyes to get the message out. "Sorry to waken you, sir. There's a call at the desk for you, sir."

Alvarez farted rudely and scowled at the boy. "Call? What do mean a call?"

The boy blushed crimson and his stupid grin widened, then he squeezed his eyes shut again. "Telephone, sir. You're wanted on the telephone."

Alvarez scratched his head. Maybe he was still dreaming, he thought. He couldn't remember ever receiving a telephone call before. He had, of course; he must have. But he couldn't remember it. He was positive he'd never taken a call in the middle of the night.

"I believe it's urgent, sir," the bellboy stammered.

"You sure it's for me?"

"Yessir. Urgent. Otherwise, we wouldn't have awakened you."

Alvarez glared at him. "All right, all right. I'll be down in a minute. Soon as I find my pants."

"Yessir." The bellboy started to hold out his hand for the customary tip, thought better of it, and backed away as if he expected to be attacked.

Alvarez grunted and slammed the door in his face. He stubbed his toe again, found and lit the lamp, pulled on his trousers and boots, and clumped downstairs. Now that he was completely awake, he thought he knew who would be calling and why.

He wasn't disappointed.

"Damnation, Alvarez! Don't you have any brains at all?" The voice on the other end sounded tinny and small, and the line crackled with static, but it was Ted Paine, all right, and he was furious. "I ought to have all three of you arrested for pulling a stunt like this. Do you understand?"

Alvarez cleared his throat. He felt his own temper rising, in part because of Paine's anger, but also because he hated talking on the telephone. A man needed to make eye contact to converse properly; any fool knew a person said as much with the eyes or a tilt of the head as with the voice, and the telephone took all that away. For a man like Alvarez, who weighed his words carefully, this gadget made of wire and wood and bits of metal was an abomination. And because he hated the thing, he always wound up talking either too loudly or too softly. Without even trying, Ted Paine already had him at a disadvantage. And the fact of the debacle at Margaret Corcoran's wasn't going to help at all.

"Are you listening, Tom?"

"Yes." His reply was so loud the desk clerk turned to look at him. Alvarez lowered his voice a notch and the clerk went back to the book he was reading. "You're right, Ted. We shouldn't have done it. We just thought Arnold should look the place over once he was sober. To see if he could come up with anything that would help the investigation, you know." He wasn't about to let on that he and Comstock had let their prisoner get away from them, even if it was the truth.

There was a pause on the other end before Paine pronounced judgment. "Bullshit!"

Alvarez heard the sharp intake of breath from the third party on the line, and he smiled in spite of the circumstances. The operator, probably a young girl, would certainly tell her superiors that the commissioner of police used vile language.

"We figured maybe he'd remember something, Ted," Alvarez said as evenly as he could. "He did, too. He said there was something missing from her room, but I don't know whether it's important or not. That's all." He waited for a response, and getting none, felt compelled to fill the silence. "We didn't think it would hurt."

"Didn't think it would hurt?" Paine exploded. "You drag my principal suspect around the scene of the crime, intimidate and interrogate our only witnesses until they're forced to seek police protection, then disappear into the night without having the common courtesy even to wait for my man, and didn't think it would *hurt*? For all you know, the sonofabitch took that pin himself when he killed the girl."

A little shudder ran through Alvarez, and he looked at the earpiece while he worked over this new bit of information. "I didn't say anything about a pin. Margaret Corcoran told you?"

"None of your damn business, you sonofabitch," Paine snapped.

"Go to hell, Commissioner Paine," Alvarez snapped back. He didn't take to being sworn at by any man. He never had permitted it, and he was too old to begin now.

Paine took a different tack. "Look, Tom, I'm sorry if I offended you. The missing trinket has no significance at all."

Even through the static on the line, Alvarez recognized the lie.

"You just don't understand," Paine continued, "how delicate this thing is. The woman is very well connected politically."

"You told me that yesterday. We all want to get to the bottom of this, you know, but I don't give a fig about politics. Not if my friend is about to be charged with a murder I'm not sure he committed."

Paine's reasonable tone evaporated. "You'd better give a fig about politics, Alvarez. This is my city, and in my city you'll do things…" Static on the line garbled the rest of what he said.

Which was just as well, Alvarez supposed.

"…going to do about it?" the voice on the line said when the static cleared.

"About what? I couldn't hear you. The line was bad."

"Bullshit."

"Go to hell," Alvarez said again.

There was a long pause, and then a hard click on the other end. Alvarez, not quite sure what to do next, held on to the receiver.

"The other party has disconnected, sir," the operator said. Her voice was thin and sweet, and she sounded much too young to be listening to two crusty men argue in the middle of the night. "Shall I attempt to reconnect, sir?"

"No, I don't think so. Thank you."

"Good night, sir."

"Good night."

Alvarez hung the receiver in its cradle. "Much obliged," he said to the desk clerk. The man looked up from the book, nodded, and returned to his reading.

Alvarez scratched himself and started to go back upstairs, but changed his mind and found a chair in the lobby where he could watch the coming dawn through the leaded glass windows on either side of the main lobby door.

He pretended to doze, but as was his habit when

something troubling needed thinking through, he let his irritation over the telephone call play itself out in his mind.

On the one hand, Paine was absolutely correct: he and Comstock had botched the job of keeping Toothacker out of mischief. But what did it matter that Margaret Corcoran had political friends if this was just a simple case of murder? And how did the bluestone brooch fit into all of this? Paine had known all about it, yet said it had no significance.

Deep in his bones Alvarez found himself wanting very much to get a look at that trinket. For the first time, he believed Arnold Toothacker.

After a time, he stretched and yawned, then pulled himself out of the chair and went to stand by the windows to get a better look at the coming of the new day. The clouds had blown away overnight, and when it came, sunrise was glorious. The velvety blackness of the sky faded first to deep lavender, then to rose, and finally to the deep, brilliant blue of the high country. He didn't see a sky like that very often in Kansas. A rime of frost had formed on the wrought-iron grillwork of the ornamental shutters and the grass in the little park across the street caught the slanting rays of white sunlight, refracting and reflecting them until both iron and grass glistened like a scattering of gemstones.

It was a perfect morning, and quiet as only the hour of daybreak can be in a big city, after the milk wagons have finished their rounds but before the working men and women leave their homes and trudge off to another day's labors.

Alvarez was still there when a black carriage marked "Denver City Police" pulled up across the street and a short, round-faced man in a long tan coat got out. Even from the distance, Alvarez could see the bulge of a big weapon under the coat. The man walked to a park bench directly opposite the hotel entrance, sat down, and waved to the carriage driver, who snapped the reins over the team's back and rumbled away.

So Ted Paine was taking no chances.

Alvarez started for his room. The desk clerk looked up from his book and smiled.

"Lovely day, ain't it, sir?" the clerk offered.

"We'll see," Alvarez said. "We'll see."

Chapter 10

I T TURNED OUT TO BE A LONG AND BORING DAY, made longer by the certainty that they were being watched. Alvarez had told Comstock about the stakeout, and the two of them had watched the park bench across the street off and on throughout the day. The short man in the duster had stayed right there until mid-afternoon, when a tall redhead with a handlebar mustache and a similar bulge under his own tan coat replaced him.

With Toothacker underfoot, Alvarez and Comstock did little more than sit around and get on each other's nerves. Alvarez spent the first part of the afternoon listening to two retired Pinkerton investigators argue about the James Gang's train-robbing methods and the last part listening to Bat Masterson and Bill Tilghman tell endless old-time yarns. How often could a man hear a blow-by-blow account of Jack Johnson's latest prizefight—or how statehood had brought a new breed of rascal to Oklahoma—before he went crazy?

By evening, all Alvarez wanted to do was get away, but

the only thing he had to look forward to was another round of too much to eat and drink. The convention was about to draw to a close, and he had nothing more to show for this trip to Denver than a case of the jitters.

Alvarez spent a half-hour in his room cleaning and oiling the Smith and Wesson, then he brushed off his black suit coat and slipped it on. The weather had turned sharply colder, and the heavy woolen garment would feel good, even in the crowd of sweating old men working hard at bringing their get-together to an end.

He was going to be very glad to leave Denver behind— assuming the matter of Arnold Toothacker didn't put a crimp in his plans. Which was a hell of a big assumption.

Paine's early-morning call still galled him, as did the police stakeout of the Drover's, and he couldn't help wondering whether the commissioner was working as hard at investigating the woman's murder as at keeping an eye on Toothacker.

He brushed again at a stubborn spot on his coat sleeve.

Maybe that wasn't fair. Paine probably was doing his best. Maybe scientific policework *was* better than the old way after all; the evidence might prove beyond a shadow of a doubt that Toothacker was guilty.

He sat on the bed and buffed his brown boots with a piece of rag. Maybe he was just fooling himself. Old age was creeping up on him, and that was a fact. Maybe he should just go home, put his feet up, and let the autumn go by and winter come on. He'd always thought his instincts would stay keen and true forever, but they hadn't. The investigative skills that had once been as natural to him as breathing had started to atrophy as soon as he'd quit using them regularly, and this business with Toothacker proved it. Almost two days had gone by since Arnold had gotten himself in trouble, and what had he or Comstock accomplished? Nothing. Once upon a time, no member of the Federal Marshal Service had ever worked harder or smarter, but what he'd done so far on this case any wet-behind-the-ears first-year man on Ted Paine's force would have done as well.

Probably better.

But then again, he'd never been a quitter—or a self-doubter, for that matter—and this was a terrible time to start. One way or another, he had to get at the truth about the killing, if only because his pride wouldn't allow him to do anything else.

Maybe he should send a telegram to his wife after dinner. It might take him a few days to finish up with this business, and she'd be looking for him day after tomorrow.

Someone knocked at the door.

That would be Comstock and Toothacker, ready to go downstairs.

"It's about time, dammit!" he growled, but he took the time to brush the last fleck of lint off the front of his coat and glance at himself in the mirror to make certain the part in his hair was straight.

He opened the door.

Something big and black moved through his field of vision just before the heavy blow slammed into the right side of his head just above the ear, but he had no time to think, to react, even to recognize what was happening. The blow set off an explosion in his head, and the world turned blazing red and he slipped out of consciousness even before his body slumped to the floor.

***

Ben Comstock bent over to tie his high-topped kidskin shoes. He was getting soft around the middle, and he felt his belt buckle digging into the roll of belly fat. He reckoned he deserved to be reminded that he was guilty of too much high living, spending too much money on kidskin and good whiskey and T-bone steaks and soft pillows. Not that he hadn't earned his right to a little easy living after all those years of making do with whang leather, rotgut, and a bit of hard ground.

He sighed and smiled at Arnold Toothacker.

Toothacker tried to return the grin but failed. He was lost within himself, as he had been for the better part of the day, and it made Comstock nervous.

It was time he snapped out of it. Past time.

Comstock wished he could turn Arnold over to Tom Alvarez and just walk away from the both of them for a few hours, but Tom had insisted they both take responsibility for Arnold during the banquet. And he couldn't argue with Alvarez's caution that there'd not be any repeat of last night's escape, since Comstock was the one who'd let Arnold get away the first time.

"I know where the brooch came from," Toothacker said so suddenly and with such conviction that Comstock jumped.

"What?"

Toothacker licked his lips and twisted his fingers together. He'd been working on this puzzle all day, but the revelation he'd seen so clearly a moment before threatened to slip away into the shadows of his addled memory. "In Pueblo." He attempted a weak smile. "It belonged to... a woman of quality."

Comstock waited for Arnold to finish the thought, but he seemed unwilling or unable to do it without prompting. "Who? Lilly Morgan?"

"No. Not her." Toothacker shook his head and frowned. "Someone else. Someone older."

"Think hard, Arnold."

Toothacker licked his lips again. "I don't know. It slips away. God, Ben, I need a drink bad."

"We'll buy you a brandy after dinner," Comstock promised. Alvarez would be furious, but he'd handle Alvarez later. "First you have to think hard about who it was you saw with the brooch."

"I could sure use a rye now."

Comstock pulled on his suitcoat. "You just try to think where you saw that brooch."

Arnold turned his gaze out the window as the shadows of early evening gathered in the park across the street. He took a deep breath and let it out like a sigh. "I think it was at a funeral. For a judge." He squeezed his eyes shut, remembering in spite of the aching hunger for alcohol. "The last territorial judge in Pueblo. Died a couple of years ago. A woman at the funeral was wearing that brooch."

"You sure it wasn't one just like it?"

"It was that one."

"Two years is a long time." And especially when you've spent it with your brain pickled in rye, Comstock said to himself.

"But I remember. Gertrude was with me, and she commented on it." He jerked a little at the sound of his wife's name, as if he were surprised the sound had come out of his own mouth.

"Then who was wearing it?"

Toothacker slumped forward until his forehead rested on the window pane. Gertrude. He could see her as she'd be when he tried to explain how he'd gotten himself into this fix: righteous, stern, strong, understanding because she had to be but disappointed in him just the same. Always disappointed. She was his strength and his salvation and a constant reminder of his shame. Why had he let her down all these years? Was it because she had the willpower he lacked? The harder he tried to be worthy of her, the more he drank, and the more he drank, the harder it was to face her every day. He heard her crying into her pillow at night, but she never once whined or complained to his face. She just took over managing their lives quietly, making sure they had clothes to wear and food to eat and a warm house to live in—but dear God, so utterly her house!—when he wasn't doing anything more than bumming drinks in the saloons. He loved her—or had loved her—but it was hard loving a saint. He missed her the way she used to be, when she had needed him more.

"Arnold, who was wearing the brooch?"

He sighed again and tried to put Gertrude out of his mind. Brooch. Where had he seen it? A woman of quality. "I don't remember exactly. The wife of someone important was wearing it. If I had a drink, I'd remember."

"Well, it's a start," Comstock said without really believing it. Some bigwig took a fancy to a young prostitute and gave her a bauble that rightfully belonged to his wife. Nothing so unusual about that. It wasn't the sort of thing someone got killed over, that was for sure.

There was a rustling noise coming from Alvarez's room, and Comstock checked his pocketwatch. Thank God.

It was time.

"You ready, Arnold?"

Toothacker straightened up slowly.

"All right, then." Comstock handed him his coat. "Let's—"

A knock on the door interrupted him. It must be Alvarez, impatient to get going.

"We're ready, Tom," Comstock called out.

Someone on the other side of the door mumbled something. It wasn't Alvarez's voice.

"Pardon?"

There was another mumble in answer.

Comstock crossed to the door. When he twisted the knob, the door exploded inward, as if some huge weight had been thrown against it. Comstock was knocked backward, lost his balance, and started to fall.

As soon as he saw the shotgun, he tried to roll to his right to get out of the way of what he knew was coming, and he almost made it.

There was a blinding flash of orange flame, and even as the flash seared his eyes, the incredible sound of two 12-gauge shells detonating at once filled his head with a crashing noise that reverberated off the walls.

Comstock felt the hot-knife stinging pain of buckshot deep in his hip and thigh as he landed hard on his back, smelled the burnt gunsmoke.

Heard the running in the hallway. Someone was running away.

Heard the whispered, strangling sound of a single word that faded away with the echoes of the gunshot: "Gertrude."

Wondered where the hell Tom Alvarez was.

And saw the blood on his kidskin shoes, on the quilt at

the end of the bed, everywhere.
But not his blood.

Chapter 11

T HE FIRST THING TOM ALVAREZ WAS AWARE OF was the spicy smell of cigar smoke. The second was the headache behind his left eye that throbbed in time to his heartbeat.

Which meant he was still alive, even if it hurt so damn badly he wasn't sure he wanted to be.

He gritted his teeth and opened his eyes slowly, but the lamplight stabbed him like a rusty hunting knife, and he squeezed his eyes against the pain. A strong hand on his arm held him gently against the goosedown pillow.

"Keep still, Tom. Just keep still and you'll be all right."

The voice was vaguely familiar, but it took more strength than he had to try to puzzle it out. His ears buzzed, and the metronome beat of the headache made everything—breathing, thinking, remembering—almost unbearable.

But he had to remember.

"Dammit, stop moving, pard!" someone said. This voice had a theatrical presence and power that he could recognize. It belonged to Bill Cody. And then he placed the other voice, as much because of the cigar smell as anything else. He inhaled deeply just to be sure of the familiar perfume of Havana tobacco. Ted Paine.

He forced his eyes open, blinked, and held them open, focusing mostly by willpower.

Paine stood over him, with Cody alongside.

"How you doin', pard?" Cody asked. Alvarez thought he saw a shadow cross Paine's face at the question, a tightening of jaw or a squinting of eye that might have been anger or impatience, but it lasted only an instant if it ever existed at all.

"Bill Tilghman found you right after the shooting," Paine said soothingly. "You took quite a whack with a blackjack or pistol butt. You've been out cold for better than two hours. Bill had you brought here, to his room."

Alvarez let the information sink in before he tried to roll onto his side and push himself upright. Nausea washed over him, receded, and returned. He decided he could live with it.

"Careful, Tom," Paine urged. "Don't overdo."

"To hell with you," Alvarez snapped through clenched teeth, and he pushed himself up and swung his legs over the side of the bed. Great blue spots swam before his eyes, but in spite of them he could make out the other old boys at the foot of the bed.

There was Wyatt Earp, tall and angular and dark, and lanky John Poe and Bill Tilghman, with the potbelly and the piercing eyes hard as a January blizzard. Bat Masterson, short, moon-faced, nearsighted, gave him a wink, but with embarrassment in his eyes.

"Glad to see you alive, Thomas," Tilghman said in his

flat Oklahoma twang.

A round-faced policeman leaning against the door cleared his throat delicately. Alvarez tried to place the policeman but couldn't. Or could he? He tried hard to decide whether he knew him from somewhere.

And then Paine's words sunk in.

"Shooting?" he asked. "What shooting?"

Bill Cody stretched out a soft hand to comfort him. "I've got some bad news for you, Tom."

"What shooting?" Alvarez demanded. His stomach was churning, but he fought off the sickness.

"One of our own is gone, Tom," Cody said, the words rolling off his tongue. "Arnold Toothacker passed on this evening about the same time some thug pistol-whipped you."

Wyatt Earp wrinkled his rat face and glared at Cody. "He didn't 'pass on,' you old coot. They cut the sonofabitch in half with a shotgun!" Earp turned to Alvarez. "Probably didn't know what hit him. Took both barrels, I'd say."

Alvarez let the air out of his lungs slowly. His headache was suddenly much worse. "Arnold's dead?"

"Gone to his great reward for certain, I'm afraid," Cody said, looking down his nose at Earp, who returned the favor with a sneer.

"Comstock. What happened to him?"

"Got winged is all," Earp said. "Took a couple of buckshot in the arse." He slapped a bony hand against his own backside. "Won't be doin' much settin' for a spell, that's for damn sure."

Ted Paine gave Earp a sharp look. "That'll be enough," he said evenly. "All of you." Alvarez saw the shadow cross his face again, and this time there was no doubt it was real.

"You sure Ben's all right?" Alvarez asked.

"The doctor's down the hall now, pulling a few pellets out of him. Then he'll be by to take another look at you. He may want to take both of you to the hospital."

"No hospitals," Alvarez growled. "I've never been in any damn hospital, and I don't plan to start now." He probed gingerly at the lump behind his right ear, on the opposite side of his head from his throbbing headache. Which meant concussion. The way old Doc Charles had explained it to him once in Abilene, the brain sloshed around inside a man's head like thick stew in a pot: he'd been struck on the right side of his skull, sending his brain slamming into the left side with enough force to knock him out. Concussions were nothing to mess with, but you generally lived through them, Doc said. Which was probably good enough under the circumstances.

"Lucky they hit you where they did," Paine said as if he could read Alvarez's mind. "A couple of inches forward and they'd have crushed the thin bones of the temple like an egg."

"Right," Alvarez said. "Damn lucky. Luckier than Arnold, anyway."

Paine's teeth ground together, and he turned the smile on the others. "Let's go, gentlemen," he said, dismissing them with the contempt he might show a common pickpocket. "Marshal Alvarez needs his rest."

Cody arched his back as if to argue, but the wind went out of him. Wyatt Earp let out a thin cackle with a dangerous edge to it. "Well," he said to no one in particular, "I don't reckon there's any sense in missing supper, is there?"

Paine stayed awhile, then left to continue the investigation of the Toothacker killing. Alvarez got up and followed him. What those two shots had done was appalling. Both barrels of a shotgun loaded with buckshot at point-blank range, and the poor sot was torn and bloodied from chin to crotch; the doctor who'd pulled the pellets out of Comstock's backside had pronounced Toothacker dead almost as an afterthought. A pair of constables took statements, rummaged around their hotel rooms, and picked buckshot out of the wall for evidence. When they finished, Ted Paine offered a perfunctory promise that there'd be a complete and scientific investigation of the crime, then hurried off to more pressing business.

Alvarez threw up once, felt better, and went looking for Comstock, who was just finishing getting patched up. Against the doctor's orders, the two of them went downstairs for a drink.

Comstock eased himself into a horsehair chair someone had dragged into the bar for him and swirled the brandy around in his glass and tossed it down. His whole left side was beginning to ache from the pellet wounds, and the brandy wasn't helping at all.

"You should have let the doctor give you something," Alvarez said.

Comstock waved it off. "I'm fine. Laudanum would just knock me out." He opened his hooded eyes a notch and them closed them again. "Looks like you could use a sawbones yourself with that goose egg alongside your head." A grin hardened into something like fury and he brought his fist down on the tabletop. "I don't know about you, but I don't much take a shine to getting shot at."

Alvarez said nothing.

"What's more, that policeman friend of yours don't seem to care any more about poor old Arnold than he would a cranky horse somebody had to put down. Mebbe less. An' whilst I'm at it, I'm damn disappointed in them sorry old excuses for lawmen we've been hanging around with." Suddenly, he was the old Comstock, as dangerous and unpredictable as a rabid wolf.

"They're soft, Ben. Like us." Alvarez didn't look up from his drink.

"I ain't soft," Comstock said fiercely. "Not by a damn sight."

Alvarez glanced at his companion, then returned his gaze to his glass, as if he might find some answers there. He had to admit the shooting had left him with a cold knot in the pit of his stomach and a clamminess that slickened the palms of his hands, but it was fear mixed with exhilaration, the excitement that danger had always triggered in him. "Maybe we've gotten too respectable," he said, glad that he didn't really believe it.

Comstock let out a little grunt as he tried to get comfortable in the chair. "All I know is, I intend to catch the bastard who did this. To get even for the pain in my own ass, if not for Arnold. So help me God!"

Alvarez considered it for a moment, then tossed down his brandy. "I heard some of the boys say we ought to get up a posse, just like we used to."

Comstock waved the bartender over for a refill. "Talk's cheap, Tom. We need doers, not talkers. Some sonofabitch killed Arnold Toothacker and damn near got us killed in the process, and I ain't sittin' still for it."

Alvarez stared deeper into his glass. "Ted Paine's boys are on the case. They'll catch the culprit."

"You haven't asked my opinion, but I think your police commissioner friend is worthless as tits on a boar hog,

Thomas." The waiter brought a fresh round. "You tell me, how did an assassin get in and out of this here hotel if Ted Paine was havin' it watched the whole damn day?"

Alvarez shrugged. "It's a big hotel."

"It ain't that big. Someone wanted Arnold out of the way. Someone killed that girl and then did him in, probably to keep him from rememberin' any more about it."

"That's what your hunches tell you?"

"Damn right."

The big party in the banquet hall began to break up. The convention was officially over, and numerous friends drifted by to say so-long or to offer embarrassed assurances of help finding whoever had gone gunning for Toothacker. Then they drifted on. Sometime tomorrow, they'd all make their way to the train station and put Denver behind them. A reporter from the *Rocky Mountain News* would be there to take pictures and write a final glowing paragraph or two about old-time exploits few of the paper's readers would remember or give a damn about, and that would be that.

Alvarez was right. They were soft.

Wyatt Earp was among the last to come by their table.

"You boys look bored," he said, exhaling breath smelling of sour whiskey and cigar into their faces. "Cody and I are going to do the town, and you're invited if you're up to it. First we're looking for women, then maybe later a poker game or some roulette." He chuckled evilly. He spoke like an educated man when he was drunk, dropping use of frontier slang the riffraff expected of him. "Masterson's coming along, too, though I don't suppose the locals are too damn keen on a proven cheater like old Bat playing cards in their town!" He laughed so hard he had a coughing fit.

Comstock leaned back in his chair away from the foul

breath. "Not tonight, Wyatt."

Earp leered at him and leaned closer. "Your ass too sore?"

"I thought you hated Bill Cody," Alvarez said evenly in hopes that Comstock wouldn't rise to the bait.

Earp grinned. "Old shithead bag of wind. Knows his women, though." He straightened up too fast and teetered on his heels as if he were about to fall over. "I got a lovely little wife, but a man's never too old…" His voice trailed off.

Comstock dismissed him with a wave of his hand. "Go on, then, Wyatt. Have a good time. We've got business to discuss."

Earp teetered even farther off plumb. "You boys're goin' to get you a pound of flesh, ain't you? Back in eighty-one, me an' Virgil an' Morgan…" He seemed to lose the thread of the story, and he licked his lips while he struggled to remember. "Where was I? Oh, yeah. Morgan was a hell of a man. Cut down in his prime. At least Toothacker had his day. You going to his funeral? The whole bunch of us is." He waved a bony finger in Alvarez's face. "You sure you don't want to come with us tonight? Bill Cody's organizing the accommodations, but it'll be a great time in spite of that old faker."

"The old faker's calling you," Alvarez said, pointing toward the lobby. Cody gave them a bow.

Earp sniffed and tried to straighten up. "See you boys later, then."

"Doubt it," Comstock said.

"Don't be so cantankerous, Benjamin. You were the one who came out of this little scrape lucky as hell," Earp said, and he gave them a little salute and wandered off.

"I thought those two hated each other," Alvarez said.

Comstock spat into the sawdust at their feet as if to get a foul taste out of his mouth. "Wyatt'll sidle up to anyone willin' to pay for the women. I'd say they deserve each other. Earp the pistol-whipping sonofabitch and Cody the biggest liar on the face of the earth. Personally, I wouldn't give either one of them a drink if they was dying of thirst."

"I will admit I never had much time for showboat people who spend all their time making themselves famous," Alvarez agreed.

"Not like us, that's for sure," Comstock sniffed. "We worked our asses off for thirty years and what'd we get for it? Sure as hell, we didn't get famous."

"But we got the job done, didn't we?" Alvarez said, tilting his head to one side and trying the words again because he liked the sound of them. "We got the job done."

Comstock's eyes slid closed as he weighed his words. "You know, Wyatt may have a handle on one thing. I sure as hell would like my pound of flesh."

The knot in the pit of Alvarez's stomach tightened, but he liked the rush of tension spreading through him. "A pound of flesh."

"We got the job done in them days, didn't we?" It wasn't a question. Comstock opened his eyes a little, and there was a shine to them even in the dim, smoky light of the saloon. He raised his glass. "So here's to Arnold, anyway, and here's to sending his killer straight to hell!"

Later, as they made their way through the lobby and up the grand staircase to their rooms, both of them saw the moon-faced policeman sprawled in an overstuffed chair with his head buried in a paper. They didn't see the other visitor waiting patiently in the shadows of the servants' entrance.

Chapter 12

IT WAS THE LAST THING ALVAREZ HAD EXPECTED.

He was up and shaving well before dawn and trying very hard to think in spite of the headache that kept him awake the two hours he'd lain in bed. His hand shook as he stropped the steel blade and drew it down his cheek, and the eyes looking back at him from the mirror above the basin were puffy and bloodshot. He felt like he was a hundred years old.

The soft tapping at the door made him jump so, he nearly cut a piece of his lip off.

Assassins; for an instant, no other thought came to mind.

He held his breath and waited. There was the tapping again.

He put the razor down, wiped off the shaving soap with a rough hotel towel, opened the bureau drawer as quietly as he could, and withdrew the Smith and Wesson.

"Sir, please open up," someone said from beyond the door. The voice was soft and young and very feminine.

Alvarez felt his chest tighten. He forced a deep, calming breath, and raised the gun, pressing himself against the wall a few inches from the door. "Who's there?" His voice cracked.

"I need to see you. Please, sir."

"I said who is it?" He held his breath, waiting for a reply.

"Please, sir, open the door." She tapped again.

He reached over with his left hand, turned the knob, and jerked the door open in one smooth motion. As the door burst inward, he crouched as low as his stiff leg would permit and swung the Smith and Wesson up to eye level. He was too slow and too clumsy; if she really had been an assassin, he would have been a dead man.

The young woman stood before him, her black-gloved hand poised to rap on the door again, her eyes suddenly wide with fright at the violence of his sudden movement and the gun aimed at her heart.

Alvarez straightened slowly, his sore leg fighting him. "Who the hell are you?" he asked. She blinked and backed up a few inches, but he reached out and snatched at the gloved hand. With a twist of his wrist, he jerked her inside and kicked the door shut. He gave her a quick once-over without lowering the gun. He guessed she was eighteen or nineteen, though she might have been somewhat older. She was very beautiful, with a soft white body leaning to plumpness; tight brown curls spilled out from under an expensive bonnet. She smelled of good perfume—a scent he recognized. It had permeated Mrs. Corcoran's house.

"You're hurting me," she whimpered, but it was more acquiescence than complaint, as if she were used to being hurt.

He let go of her hand and lowered the Smith and Wesson, but kept his thumb on the hammer just in case.

She smiled thinly and brushed one brown curl away from her face. "I'm sorry to disturb you, sir." She was trembling.

"What do you want?"

"I've been waiting all night," she said. "I didn't want the police officers who were watching you to see me, so I waited for a shift change."

He shook his head, trying to understand. "Tell me who you are and why you're here."

She turned her eyes away from the weapon. "My name is Juanita," she said quietly. "I'm from Mrs. Corcoran's, although I suppose you know that already."

"So?"

"I'm a friend of Mr. Hill. That is, Mrs. Corcoran's butler."

"I don't know who you mean."

"Ulysses," she said.

"So? What do you want with me?"

"I… I have something for you."

"What?"

She looked down at her dainty shoes and then up at him. "It's something that belonged to a friend of mine. Something I think you're looking for," she said so softly he scarcely heard her. Then, slowly, she raised her fingers to her throat and delicately pulled her lace collar aside just enough to reveal a pin of dark blue stone set in a border of silver filigree.

Alvarez and Comstock headed out at first light.

Paine's man had the Drovers lobby covered, but they

slipped down the back stairs and into the alley, where they talked a junkman into giving them a lift. It was an hour past sunrise when the junkman's rattletrap buckboard pulled to a stop in another alley, this time three blocks from Margaret Corcoran's, and let them off.

They walked from there, slipping through the frosted autumn weeds toward the south bank of the Platte.

The city was slow to awaken on a Sunday morning. The usual clatter of streetcars and horses' hooves and the occasional roar of a motorcar were missing. The riverbank was doubly quiet. Crows awoke in their roosts and scolded the two men as they passed, and something small and furry skittered out of their way in the thick tangle of grass and willow roots, but for the most part the morning was so still they could hear the river sliding over the soft mud banks.

When they came up behind Margaret Corcoran's gray house, they stopped and caught their breaths. Comstock looked pasty white, but Alvarez couldn't tell whether it was from the half-light of the thicket or a real change in his complexion.

"You all right?"

Comstock waved it off. "I may have ripped a stitch. Don't worry about me. Let's get on with this."

"You're sure you're okay?"

Comstock glared at him and spat into the soft earth. "Come on, Tom. Time's wastin'. This is your party, you know."

Alvarez leaned against a sturdy willow to take some of the weight off his leg. His own heart was pounding from the excitement and exertion. "Right." He checked the height of the sun above the eastern horizon against his pocketwatch and searched the weeds for a handful of pebbles.

"It's time," he said.

Comstock muttered something about this being the hard way to get Ulysses' attention, but Alvarez only hefted a rock. They had to talk to Ulysses, but a house full of whores was sure to raise a ruckus over two old men stomping into their kitchen. Margaret Corcoran would have the law down on them in nothing flat, and Alvarez wasn't itching for a fight with the police. He rubbed his hawk nose with the back of his hand and crept closer to the back of the house.

His first throw fell short, but the second slapped against the clapboard with a dull *thwack*. He managed several more solid hits, then slid down the bank to where Comstock waited among the willows.

Comstock was already pointing toward the house.

Ulysses, barefoot and struggling to pull his suspenders up over a dazzling white union suit, was coming around the corner. He saw Alvarez, growled something, and broke into a trot toward them with his head down and his arms swinging in a powerful loping gait. He was only twenty feet away when Alvarez pulled his old gun and touched an index finger to his lips to make the necessary point. Ulysses stopped in mid-stride and drew himself up to argue, but when Alvarez thumbed back the revolver hammer and lifted the weapon to aim it squarely between the butler's eyes, the fight went out of him. Comstock eased up alongside, grabbed a handful of union suit, and pulled him farther down the bank toward the murmuring river.

Alvarez, coming along behind, took special care as he nudged Ulysses along with the business end of the Smith and Wesson pressed against his spine.

Comstock led the way into the undergrowth until he found a deadfall cottonwood. "Will this do?"

Alvarez nodded and motioned to Ulysses to sit. "No more cat-and-mouse like the other night. We want answers this time." He aimed the cocked revolver at a point on the white union suit just an inch below the hunchback's chin.

Ulysses gave them both a haughty stare. "I don't know anything," he said almost casually.

"Our friend Arnold Toothacker was killed last night, and Ben here took some buckshot. We don't much cotton to things like that, and I think you know who did it, Mr. Hill. Hill is your name, isn't it?"

The blood seemed to drain from the man's face, and he sucked in his breath just a little. "I don't know anything," he repeated.

Alvarez stabbed the gun at him. "What's the matter? Surprised to hear Toothacker was killed?" He straightened up. "I think you'll tell us a good deal more than we know already, or we'll turn you over to the police."

"On what charge?"

"Theft. Or something a good deal worse."

"I'm no thief, sir." He bent over and rubbed his freezing feet. He was shaking.

Without letting the muzzle of the gun move off his target, Alvarez reached into his coat pocket with his left hand and pulled out a small white bundle, which he tossed to Comstock. "Oh, I think you are. And maybe something a good deal worse," he repeated,

Comstock unwrapped the little package carefully and held its contents out just beyond Ulysses Hill's grasp.

He stared at the small object and his jaws worked together so furiously the other two could hear his teeth grinding. Perspiration stains spread across Hill's chest and darkened the union suit beneath his arms. "I should wring her damned neck," he said almost to himself.

The dappled light filtering through the cottonwood leaves caught the object and played off its smooth surface. The soft breeze had died, and the day was warming with the rising sun.

Alvarez took the brooch from Comstock and wrapped it in the handkerchief. "But you love the girl," he said. "Or so she says. According to her, you plan to marry her once you've stolen away Margaret Corcoran's clientele and set up the grandest house in Denver. Juanita seems to love you, though I can't see why. But she says she doesn't want to be associated with a thief… or a murderer."

"I'm no murderer," Hill said evenly, but he clasped his hands tightly in front of him, his eyes fixed on his white knuckles.

"What about Lilly Morgan?"

A little shudder ran through him. "I didn't kill her."

Alvarez hefted the Smith and Wesson, making a show of it. "I think you did. Or you know who did."

Hill said nothing.

Ben Comstock leaned forward close to Hill. "Dammit, Thomas, he's lying."

Hill gave him a withering look, his black eyes ablaze. "Go to hell."

It was a mistake. In one smooth motion, Comstock slipped his right hand into his coat and withdrew a Colt double-action .38. Hill saw the gun and backed away, but not in time. Comstock brought the barrel up swiftly, raking Hill's chin with the blade sight as he squeezed the trigger to full cock.

"Ben…" Alvarez protested.

Comstock snorted and held the muzzle against Hill's

throat. "You tell us what you know or I'll blow your damn head off, you snakeshit sonofabitch!"

Hill gulped and touched the scrape on his chin with the back of his hand.

"Ben, don't do it." Alvarez took a step toward the two.

Comstock whirled on Alvarez. "You back off, Thomas. Remember, this was your idea. Well, I been shot and a good man's dead, and I aim to find out why!" He swung back to Hill and jabbed him so hard with the .38 he nearly fell over backward. "Now you tell us what happened or you'll be crow bait, God damn your hide!"

"Now, Mr. Hill, perhaps you should start at the beginning," Alvarez said.

Hill licked his lips and looked into Alvarez's eyes. The wind had gone out of him. "All right," he said slowly, wiping his palms on his legs. "It's true your friend didn't kill the girl."

"I knew that much!" Comstock hissed. "Tell me something I don't know."

Hill's misshapen body seemed to sag under its own weight. Real fear showed in his eyes. "I killed her. Someone paid me. Your friend showed up and I figured since he was dead drunk and wouldn't remember anything, I could make it look like he did it. But I didn't have anything to do with his killing. Honest."

"Who paid you?" Alvarez asked.

Hill hesitated.

"Go on, damn you!" Comstock snapped.

He started to say something but stopped, cocking his head.

"Damn your ass," Comstock said. "You better—"

But Alvarez heard it, too, and shushed him, jerking his

head in the direction of the Corcoran place. Through the birdsong and the slow buzzing of lazy autumn insects came the faint crackle of voices. Male voices, barking orders.

"Ted Paine's boys!" Alvarez whispered. "They discovered we were gone or followed the girl."

Comstock leered at their prisoner. "Maybe that ain't so bad. Now that we've got us a murderer, we can turn him over to your friend Paine!" He grinned and pulled the revolver away from Hill's neck, lowering the hammer carefully. "Then he can start doing the damn job he's paid to do!"

Hill blinked and rubbed at the little round mark on his neck where the barrel had been. "Don't count on it."

"Why the hell not?"

Hill hesitated, and a trace of bravado crept back into his voice. "Because he's the one who hired me to kill the girl."

Comstock bellowed, "Bullshit."

The dead black eyes found Comstock's and held them. "You want to take a chance to find out?" The commotion at the house was growing louder. "If I'm right, you two are dead men."

"So are you," Comstock said. "*If* you're right." But he heard the commotion, too, and began backing off, giving himself some room to get away.

Alvarez was ahead of him. He stuffed the bluestone brooch into his pocket while he kept watch up the trail, as if expecting to be discovered at any second. "We better think this thing through, Ben." He waved the gun in Ulysses Hill's face one last time. "We'll be back," he said. "We still got business with you."

"If you can find me," Hill said under his breath, but he

was already moving deeper into the concealment of the undergrowth.

The two old lawmen set off through the tangle of weeds and willows, following the river away from Ulysses Hill and the Corcoran place and the unwelcome visitation of the Denver police.

It took then an hour to find their way to the redbrick canyons of downtown. The going was tough, and both were grim-faced and silent as they limped along. The day was growing warm, even for September, and the air had a heaviness to it like summer air with a thunderstorm brewing. Comstock fell behind from time to time, and Alvarez grew impatient waiting and moved on ahead, keeping to a steady pace that was easy on his stiff leg.

He reached into his pocket as he walked and fingered the brooch, running through the pertinent facts, worrying over them. Was Hill telling the truth? He probably had killed Lilly Morgan, but could it have been at Ted Paine's bidding? He doubted it. More likely, he'd killed her for reasons of his own and stolen the bauble. Still, if that were the case, why had Arnold Toothacker been killed? Why hadn't Paine shown more interest in looking for the brooch? And why were they being watched now that Toothacker was dead? Alvarez hoped they'd have another chance to talk to Ulysses, but he wouldn't bet his life on it.

As they walked, he looked at every intersection for loitering men in tan dusters and kept watch over his shoulder to assure himself they weren't being followed. He saw no one, but it didn't make him feel any safer.

They approached the Drovers cautiously, and it was a good thing. There was no mistaking Paine's man: he was making small talk with the hotel doorman. Fortunately, he had his back turned to the park, and the two men slipped into the shade of a big oak.

Comstock squatted down next to Alvarez. "How the hell are we going to get past him?" His voice was thin and tight, and his trousers were black and sticky with drying blood.

"You ripped yourself open."

Comstock grunted. "I'll be all right. Leg's just stiffening up."

"Bullshit. You're bleeding like a stuck hog."

Comstock laughed thinly. "We got other things to worry about. I'd say right now Denver's a damn dangerous place for us to be."

"You don't believe that story about Paine paying to have the girl killed, do you?"

"Hell if I know. But Arnold and that girl are dead, I'm busted open, and the local law's trying to tie us up tighter'n a tick. You tell me what's going on."

"Shit," Alvarez said. He looked at Comstock, then at the hotel, and watched the young constable in the duster for several minutes while he thought. "We'll never get by that boy yonder. My guess is the minute he sees us, we'll be under arrest."

Comstock shifted uneasily. "And you have the brooch on you. They'll charge theft, sure as hell."

Alvarez brought the pin out of his pocket and studied the situation.

"We don't have much choice," he said. He knelt at the base of the tree and scraped away some of the soft earth from around an old root, slid the brooch into the depression, covered it, and tamped down the dirt.

"There," he said. "In case we get stopped. Now come on. There's someone we need to see who may be able to help us out, or at least answer some more questions."

"Who?"

Alvarez couldn't help a sly grin. "The most famous man in Denver."

Chapter 13

ULYSSES HILL RAPPED SOFTLY ON THE DOOR. Twice, a pause, then three times more. The usual signal. He twisted his misshapen body to get a good look up and down the darkened hallway to assure himself none of the other girls heard him before he rapped out the signal again. He'd successfully avoided the police by hiding in the willow thicket until they'd gone, and he was determined not to be discovered now, even by Margaret Corcoran. Not until he was finished.

First, he had to see Juanita.

Perhaps it would have been wiser to pretend he was an ordinary gentleman caller: he had no assurance whatever that she'd open the door to him after what had happened. She'd always been afraid of him—a fear he'd cultivated for his own purposes—and she'd be doubly afraid now, after stealing the brooch and tattling to those old bastards.

For a moment, he felt like strangling her, but he succeeded in keeping his anger in check. He was in enough trouble as it was.

He rapped out the sign a third time.

The door opened a crack and he pushed it open another inch or two, but a security chain held it firmly in place. He wanted to bull his way inside, ripping the chain out of the doorframe like a summer cyclone tearing up a willow sapling, but he took a deep breath and forced himself to stay calm.

"Let me in, Juanita," he said easily.

"No."

"Come on, darling. Let me in." He laid on the Southern charm.

She came to the door and pressed her face into the two-inch gap without opening it.

"Please. I'm not going to hurt you." He could see that she'd been crying; her eyes were red and puffy, and there was a long purple bruise on her cheek. That would be from Margaret Corcoran's cane. The police would have told Maggie that they'd spotted Juanita coming from the hotel, and Maggie would have been only too happy to strike out at the cheap tart who dared to bring the police down on her peaceful Sunday morning. Especially since it was Juanita. His Juanita.

"The police were here looking for you," she whispered, chewing on her lip nervously.

"No, they weren't. They were here looking for those two old men. The ones you went to see."

She blinked and looked away. "I didn't do it," she lied, shuffling her feet. "I didn't go to those men. It was one of the others."

He took a deep breath and forced a smile. "It's not important." His own lie sounded much more convincing than hers. "Let me in so we can talk."

She chewed on her lip some more and shook her head slowly. "No. Leave me alone."

He leaned his weight into the door, pushing hard against the security chain.

"No. Stay out!" Juanita jumped back from the door and started to whimper. "Stay out."

He pushed again, and the chain groaned. "It's not important, darling. Just let me in," he said softly, soothingly.

"Stay out! I'll call Mrs. Corcoran!" Her eyes were wild with panic.

He put his shoulder into the door in earnest. "She won't help you. She hates you."

"Stay out!" Her fear was almost strangling her, but she was loud enough to risk bringing other girls into the hall to see what was going on.

He gave a quick, hard thrust and the screw holding the chain tore free from the beechwood frame. The door swung wide, and he nearly fell into the room. Juanita leaped away from him and crossed to the far wall, where she crouched down against the head of her bed. Her breath was coming in sobs.

"Shut up!" He took two long steps across the room and grabbed her shoulders in his big hands. Her legs went limp and she struggled to get away, but not much.

"Don't," she cried, holding her arms up over her face. "Don't hit me!"

He lifted her as easily as if she were a rag doll and held

her face just inches from his own. "Why the hell did you do it? You stole it from me, didn't you, you little tramp." She cringed and shook her head violently, but he only held her tighter. "Why did you steal that brooch?"

She gulped and started to cry. "Tell me you didn't kill her. Please. You didn't kill her, did you?"

He froze stock-still for a moment, not even breathing. He had an urge to slam her against the wall to make her pay for her crime.

Or was it his crime?

He put her down, releasing her almost tenderly. "Damn you, girl! It wasn't any of your business."

She sniffed back the tears. "I… didn't want… I mean, she was killed. It was Lilly's and then she was killed and then you had it." She took a deep breath that was more spasm than voluntary effort. "You had the brooch those two men were looking for. You stole it or someone gave it to you. It was like blood money or something."

"I didn't kill her," he said.

"I thought you loved me," she sniffed. The look of wild animal fear had faded from her eyes, leaving petulance in its place.

"You were different from the others," he said. He bent over her and stroked her hair, but she jerked herself away. "I wanted so much for the two of us. And now you've gone and got me killed." He grabbed a fistful of hair and twisted it hard, and she let out a little squeak that was a mixture of fear and surprise.

"You do know you've gotten me killed, don't you?" he said almost gently. Then he turned and loped out of her room; he knew in his bones he was out of time.

Margaret Corcoran found him barely five minutes later as he threw the last of his belongings into his worn carpetbag. She leaned on her cane in the doorway to his room, her thick body blocking his exit.

A far-off booming rolled down the hallway and past him; someone was pounding on the front door, and the insistence of it sent a tremor through him. Only the police or someone coming to settle a score over a botched deal knocked that way.

"Get the door, Ulysses," Margaret Corcoran said acidly.

"Get it yourself," he said. He slammed a hairbrush and razor into the bag and snapped it shut.

He thought of Juanita again, but he thought as well of the little nickel-plated revolver in his pocket. It was just the sort of pimp gun he had always hated, but now he found the awkward way it slapped his side strangely comforting.

The woman glared back at him. "Insolence. In all our years together, I never knew you to be insolent."

The hammering at the door grew louder.

"There's a first time for everything. Now get out of my way."

She thumped her cane angrily on the oak floor. "You will not talk to me that way! Now, why are you leaving? Or do I know already?"

He said nothing.

"Explain yourself!" She thumped again.

He grasped the bag and swung it off the bed. It was surprisingly light; he had very little to show for a dozen years with Margaret Corcoran. He suppressed an urge to swing at her, to knock her out of his way. She still had a sort of magical power over him, even after all these years, and he recognized it for what it was: gratitude, in spite of everything. He loathed her, and yet he was grateful, as he had been ever since she'd taken him off the streets of Memphis and trained him to be her personal valet. In the beginning, she'd made fun of him in front of her clientele, but later, when arthritis had twisted her own limbs and he'd grown more proficient at running her house, she'd stopped the joking and they'd become lovers of sorts, then business partners at her insistence. She'd always said half the place was his, and he'd believed her; but savvy woman that she was, she'd delayed putting their agreement in writing; and, anyway, in the last few years the business had gone into a genteel decline as the society ladies put increasing pressure on their businessman husbands to clean up Denver's bawdy houses. They'd kept up pretenses better than most, but now it was too late.

"I don't owe you an explanation," was all he could say. He owed her everything, and he owed her nothing, and he was helpless before her.

"I had police officers rummaging around in here this morning, tearing this place apart as if I were a common criminal! When I needed you, you were nowhere to be found, and now you're leaving. For that, I'm owed more than an explanation!" She slammed the cane into the floor twice more for emphasis.

He stood before her, challenging her to get out of his way, but she didn't back down. "They were looking for those two old lawmen," he said through clenched teeth.

"What made them look here?" Her face was tight, and her eyes were mere slits of watery blue.

"I don't know. They'd been here before. Maybe the police thought they'd come back."

"Were they correct?"

He said nothing.

"Were you with them?"

He spit out the answer. "Yes." It was more answer than she deserved. His grip tightened on the satchel. The pounding was getting louder, but he could hear the pounding of his own heart over it.

"Why were you with them?" she demanded.

"They waylaid me."

She laughed in his face. "They laid a trap for you, that's what they did. Your little Juanita went to them and led them here." She said the girl's name as if the sound of it disgusted her. Her eyes were alive with jealousy. "She did, you know. I saw her go, and I saw her come back. And then when those two old bastards showed up, they managed to scare you so badly you're running away. That's what happened, isn't it?" She leaned toward him, close enough for him to smell the staleness of her breath, the sourness of yesterday's perfume.

"I'm not running." His breath caught in his throat; he ached to swing the bag into her white, puffy face but couldn't will his muscles to do the deed.

She saw his weakness and laughed again with such force that little droplets of sour spittle hit his face. "I caught your little tramp when she came in and made her tell, and I whipped her for it, and I'll whip you as well for bringing this shame into my house!" she said, biting off the words one at a time. The purple veins in her temple throbbed with each word.

He reached deep within himself for the strength to raise the satchel and swing it at her. She saw the blow coming but only grinned in the face of it as it knocked her down. He swung again, but even before the blow landed he heard the splintering of the front door and the angry voices of men in the front hall.

He dropped the valise and turned, looking for some way out. His room had only one window, curtained in velvet and high up on the wall. There was no other way out.

"You killed that Pueblo girl, didn't you? You killed her, and now you've ruined me!" she shrieked.

In two strides he was at the bed, shoved it against the wall and climbed up on it, pulling back the velvet curtain, hoisting himself up to the sill on powerful arms. The window was locked. He dropped back onto the bed, jerked off the coverlet, wrapped it around his right arm, and leaped at the window, swinging his padded fist at the pane as he jumped. The glass shattered; he caught the sill with his forearm, felt the shards pierce his skin, ignored the pain, and pulled himself upward, squeezing his hump through the small space and letting his momentum carry the rest of him through the window.

The last thing he heard before he fell was the woman's hysterical screaming, calling him a murderer.

He hit the ground in the soft grass of the north side of the house. He stood up, testing for injuries; he was sore and bleeding, but there were no broken bones. He dropped the coverlet and headed around to the front of the building.

What he saw there stopped him cold: Theodore Paine, with a black cigar clamped tightly in his grim mouth, pacing the curb while his men ransacked Margaret Corcoran's place.

God, he knows, Ulysses Hill thought. He's come to kill me.

He turned on his heel and trotted toward the river. As he ran, he felt the slapping of the little revolver against his leg.

Chapter 14

THE TROLLEY TOOK THEM ACROSS TOWN, where the conductor pointed out Louisa Cody's brownstone home. Once they'd assured themselves the place wasn't being watched, they knocked on the front door, and a maid let them into the foyer and summoned the old scout, who appeared some minutes later in a tattered robe and slippers and showed them into a gloomy green-draped library just off the parlor.

It was apparent that Louisa had permitted her husband to outfit this room to suit his own tastes, but the place had an unmistakable feminine feel in spite of the mostly masculine accoutrements. A repeating rifle with ornate silver filigree on the breech hung on the mantel below an oil painting of Cody himself mounted on a prancing Appaloosa; a stuffed buffalo head looked down from one wall and a ten-point elk from another. A fine, beaded buckskin shirt adorned a tailor's dummy in the far corner, and a sawhorse across the room cradled a hand-tooled saddle with pommel and cantle trimmed in grizzly fur. The place smelled of sage and dust and tanned skins and spilled whiskey, yet underneath there was the cloying subversive scent of rose petals and talcum. Cody was known to prefer the open spaces of his homes in Nebraska and Wyoming, but it was common knowledge as well that Louisa didn't share his love of such rustic habitats and dragged him to Denver as often as she could. Rumor had it that it was her way of getting back at him for the ugly divorce scandal of several years earlier.

He settled himself gently into a leather armchair and motioned to them to do the same, then lit a kerosene lamp on the table by his chair. It was a woman's lamp with a delicate hand-painted glass globe, and it didn't help much.

Alvarez cleared his throat. "Thank you for seeing us, Colonel," he said, but Comstock only made a face.

Cody seemed not to notice. He sprawled a little, easing one leg up over the arm of his chair and pulling the robe closed over his paunch. His long gray-blond hair was snarled, and tobacco juice had stained the corners of his mustache and dribbled down into his chin whiskers. He gave his two callers a gracious, false smile that was cut short by a grimace, and he eased his legs a little farther apart.

"Prostate trouble, I'm afraid, gentlemen," he said by way of explanation. "The curse of too many hard days in the saddle." He gave Comstock a long look. "I'd say you could use a doctor, my friend."

Comstock sniffed impatiently. "Don't worry about me. Let's get down to business."

Cody shifted his weight in his chair again. "By all means," he said icily. "What is it you gentlemen want of me?"

Alvarez gave Comstock a reproachful glance and took a

deep breath and began. "We seem to be in trouble, Colonel. We're apparently wanted men."

The old scout's eyes opened a little wider. "Why?"

Alvarez explained about the theft of the brooch and how it came into their possession, though he was careful to leave out Hill's claim that Paine had paid him to do the killing. He finished by explaining how he'd hid the brooch, but not where.

Cody ran his fingers through his matted hair. "Where are my manners? Do either of you gentlemen want some refreshment? I have an open bottle of good sour mash."

Comstock mumbled and shifted his weight purposely so a new red stain seeping along his pant leg would soak into the satin chair cover.

"We're fine," Alvarez said.

"As you wish." Cody watched Comstock and started to comment about the blood but changed his mind. "I still don't see what I can do."

"What can you tell us about what happened when the girl was killed?"

Cody flushed, and he lowered his voice to an urgent whisper. "Lord, Tom, I'd be obliged if you wouldn't mention that. Mrs. Cody isn't at home, but there are servants—"

Alvarez interrupted him. "I'm sorry, Colonel. It's important. Two people are dead."

Cody nodded gravely as he gave it some thought. Neither of the other two could tell whether he was just playacting for them. "I can't tell you anything I haven't told the police already," he said finally. "I was indisposed at the time, as you know."

"Then just tell us whether you recognized any of Mrs. Corcoran's gentleman callers."

A shocked look crossed the old man's eyes. He sniffed and wiped at his mustache with the back of a slender white hand. "There were gentlemen there who are known to me. That's quite true," he said, hesitantly, weighing each word as if to judge which one would trap him into saying something best left unsaid.

"Who were they, Bill?"

Cody leaned toward them, his eyes gone bloodshot with sudden anger, his robe falling open to reveal sparse white chest hair. "Now see here, that's a question one gentleman doesn't ask another! There's a certain code that must be honored!"

Alvarez backed off a little. "All right, Colonel, no offense intended. It's just that a U.S. marshal can't afford to be a gentleman all the time. This is murder. Manners don't enter into it."

"Manners are essential in the conduct of any business," Cody sniffed. "If you don't believe that, we have no reason to continue this conversation!"

Now Alvarez lost his temper. He shot out of his seat, towering over Cody. "Whoever bludgeoned that girl was no gentleman, and you and I both know it wasn't Arnold Toothacker. If you must know, Ulysses Hill says he was paid to kill the girl and made it look like Arnold's doing. If he was telling the truth, we want to know who paid him. We also want to know who killed Arnold and why. Ben's walking around with buckshot in his hindquarters and I've got a knot on my head the size of a goose egg, and no gentleman did that, either." He leaned closed to Cody. "And I want to know why Ted Paine seems a hell of a lot more interested in what we're doing than he does in catching the culprit," Alvarez added, letting each word drop like a stone between them. "So I don't give a damn about violating a gentleman's sacred code of silence."

The old scout's eyes narrowed, and he glanced from Alvarez to Comstock. He pulled a handkerchief out of his robe pocket and blew his nose with a loud honk. He was outnumbered. "What do you want to know?" he asked softly.

"Just tell us who was there," Alvarez said, and he leaned back in his chair to give Cody some space again. "And whether any of them have enough political power to get the Denver police to do their bidding."

Cody tapped one long index finger against his temple. "Political power?"

"Just tell me," Alvarez said.

The old scout thought about it. "There were business people there for the most part. Ordinary men. Not the sort who could get the constabulary to do their bidding, if you know what I mean." He paused and took a breath, but didn't go on.

"No one?"

Cody eased himself out of his chair and began to pace the room. "No. There was no one of that sort there."

"You're certain?"

He paused. "Maggie did mention someone to me. Someone she'd seen earlier in the day."

"Who?"

He stopped pacing. "An important man from Pueblo. A big man in Democratic circles. She said he was with Police Commissioner Paine."

Comstock sat bolt upright in his chair and Alvarez felt a little thrill of anticipation run up his spine. "Tell us more," Alvarez said.

"I lose track of Colorado politics, I'm afraid," Cody said. He was facing the window, and as he spoke his voice slipped naturally into the cadence of the theater. "I've heard he's interested in running for governor, but that may be idle rumor."

"Do you know him?"

Cody nodded. "For fifteen years, maybe. Not closely, you understand. I know thousands of people from Her Majesty Queen Victoria to…"

"Go on," Alvarez prodded. "Tell me about *him*."

"Not much to tell. He's a builder. A man who makes things happen. The sort of man Colorado needs. That's all."

"He was with Paine?"

Cody turned and smiled awkwardly and his voice trailed off. "That's what Maggie told me."

Alvarez was up and pacing the room himself. "Hill told us it was Paine who'd paid him to kill the girl."

The old scout turned back to the window, pulled aside the heavy green drapery, and opened the venetian blinds. Yellow sunlight filtered through the slats. "Interesting," he said.

Alvarez caught the inflection. "What?"

"Maybe nothing," Cody said. "Paine is a very efficient police officer. Very thorough. He's been good for Denver, I'm told. But he dances to the tune of any man with enough money or connections to keep him living well." Cody was ghostly pale against the striped light. "I've never liked him, so I suppose I'm willing to believe the worst about him."

Alvarez felt the hot blood of embarrassment rise to his face.

Cody paid no attention. "I don't know whether you'll believe this," he said, "but I do feel responsible for what happened to Toothacker. He drank too much, but which of us doesn't? He was a good man. A damn sight better'n the bootlickers who pass for lawmen these days. If you know what I mean." He returned to his chair, settling into it gingerly to hold off the stabbing pain in his groin. "There's something else you probably should know. The coffin holding your friend's body is leaving for Pueblo on a midnight train. I'm told the widow has made final arrangements for the funeral, and Commissioner Paine is leading our official Denver delegation. I'm in the party myself."

"Earp told us," Comstock said.

Buffalo Bill nodded gracefully. "Ah, yes, Earp. A difficult man. But that's beside the point. Were I you, I'd be damn careful around town today," Cody said. He smiled faintly, as if he were suddenly pleased with himself. "For what it's worth, I'll do what I can to help you."

Alvarez offered him his hand. "It's worth a lot, I'd say."

Chapter 15

ALVAREZ AND COMSTOCK SPENT THE AFTERNOON in a seedy saloon on the fringes of downtown while Ben knocked back whiskeys to dull the pain in his leg. Cody had told them he was supposed to accompany Toothacker's body to the train station as part of his responsibilities in the delegation of honor; in the meantime, he'd try to figure a way to get them out of town without running afoul of the law. The rendezvous was set for Union Station around eleven-thirty. But be careful, he said—the place would surely be watched.

Clouds swept in from the mountains in late afternoon on a quickening wind, and the lamplighters were out early on their rounds. Alvarez had not planned to go back to the Drovers to retrieve the brooch until dark, but with the change in the weather, he chanced it. He walked the six blocks with his head pulled into the collar of his coat against the blustery weather, and even so, only narrowly missed being spotted by the round-faced officer he'd seen at the foot of his bed the night before. The little man carried his shotgun out in the open, and Alvarez couldn't help wondering whether he had a blackjack under his coat as well. Perhaps the assassin did not have any trouble at all getting into the hotel because he was there all along.

Alvarez watched the police for a few minutes, dug up the pin, and returned to the saloon. Then he and Comstock ate a quick saloon supper of corned beef, cabbage, and pickled eggs, and discussed their options for the fourth or fifth time. There were damned few. They were in absolute agreement that they had to get to Ted Paine, but it'd be suicide to try on his ground. Pueblo would be their best bet, but they couldn't just hop a train. Somehow, they had to get there without letting Paine's men grab them.

Well, maybe Cody was figuring that out for them.

At eight o'clock, they found Comstock a run-down faro parlor a half mile down the tracks from the depot, where he could wait with some cheap thundergut to take the edge off the throbbing in his backside. Alvarez went on to the station, being careful to keep to the back alleys.

By the time the hearse bearing Toothacker's body was due to arrive, Alvarez was standing in the shadows of a darkened warehouse across the street.

The gaslights above the great stone arches cast a warm yellow glow over the bustle of traffic around the depot, but the sharp wind carried the wet-wool smell of snow, and in the darkness it was freezing. Alvarez hunkered down and leaned into the damp brick of the warehouse wall to rest his throbbing leg.

From where he stood, he could see two police wagons waiting while several men in long tan dusters paced up and down the broad boardwalk. The big clock high above the wide central entrance struck eleven.

He shifted his weight again to keep the blood flowing to his bad leg. The shrill whistle of a locomotive came to him from behind the depot, followed by the deep groan of the drivers turning, first slowly and then faster and faster until the sound was lost in the metallic rumble of steel wheels on the rails. When the whistle sounded again, it was lower in tone and some distance away. Eastbound, Alvarez guessed: the train he would be riding if he were going home to the warmth of his little house in Wichita. He shook his head at the irony. There was little chance of getting home that way tonight. Or anytime soon, he supposed.

The train sounds faded away, leaving only the clip-clop of many shod hooves on the cobblestones. Then he heard the rattle of a wagon.

The hearse was drawn by four matching black geldings. It was an ornate affair with brass lanterns, silver work on the sides, and black crepe draperies behind real glass windows. Probably the fanciest rig Arnold Toothacker had ever ridden in, Alvarez guessed. The driver pulled up in front of the stone arches and climbed down off the box and said something to one of the policemen. The horses stamped and shook their harness. One huge black gelding shat in the street, and its dung steamed in the cold night air.

Alvarez waited.

Five minutes. Then fifteen.

A porter appeared with a handcart and left it at the rear of the hearse.

Another police wagon rolled up ten minutes later with the pallbearers, and even from across the street, Alvarez recognized them as they lined up to remove the coffin. Ted Paine was there, puffing on a good cigar. Bat Masterson stood beside him, with lanky Wyatt Earp on the other side.

Potbellied Bill Tilghman, in his white high-crowned hat, stood next to dark old John Poe. Only Cody was missing. One of the undertaker's men moved in to make a sixth, and when Paine gave the orders, the men leaned into their work and slid the coffin out of the hearse and onto the handcart. Paine barked another order and one of the policemen disappeared into the depot, returning moments later with several porters.

William Frederick Cody chose that moment to make his appearance in a smart black buggy pulled by a high-stepping bay. As the buggy pulled to a stop in a pool of yellow lamplight, Alvarez got a good look at Cody's high white hat, the little white goatee, and the expensive chesterfield coat. Ted Paine strode up to the buggy and said something sharp that Alvarez couldn't hear, but he did hear the old scout laugh clearly enough.

"You better be playing straight, you old sonofabitch," he said under his breath, and he leaned farther back into the shadows.

Cody climbed down from the driver's seat slowly, favoring himself, and gave them all a deep bow. Earp guffawed, and Cody clapped him on the shoulder, then took his place at the head of the little entourage and led them into the depot. The porters picked up the tongue of the handcart and followed, pulling what was left of Arnold Toothacker unceremoniously into the Denver train station.

It was just past midnight when they reappeared. They shook hands all around, and Earp, Masterson, Poe and Tilghman climbed into their wagons and rumbled off. Cody started for his buggy, but Paine restrained him and they exchanged words, with Paine gesturing wildly. A train whistle blew and the low rumble of a locomotive pulling away spoiled any chance Alvarez had to hear snatches of the conversation, but he could guess what they were talking about anyway; instinctively, he laid his hand on the cold steel of the old Smith and Wesson. Cody freed himself of the commissioner at last and climbed laboriously into his buggy and snapped the whip over the bay's back. Paine stood in the street for a few minutes, then crossed the boardwalk and disappeared into the interior of the station.

Alvarez forced his cold-stiffened limbs into motion. He hurried down the alley, cut through a warehouse yard empty except for some scavenging rats that scurried away at his approach, and followed another cobblestone street for two blocks. Tall redbrick warehouses loomed on either side like some unnatural dark canyon. He rounded a corner and found himself practically nose-to-nose with Cody's bay.

"Wondered if you were coming this way, pard," Cody said from his perch on the buggy seat. There was tension in his voice. The old man had a buffalo robe over his knees, and Alvarez couldn't help wondering if there was a long gun under the hide.

Alvarez backed up two steps to give himself some maneuvering room in case he needed it. "I saw you back there. At the depot."

"I figured." Cody flicked the reins lightly and the bay took two steps forward, closing the distance between them. "Paine's beside himself looking for you, all right. Got some of his boys scouring the hotels and saloons, and they're watching all the main roads out of town. Said he'd called down to Pueblo to tell 'em to keep an eye open just in case you managed to get aboard a southbound freight. He's got so many men on the rail yards tonight a dog tick couldn't get past 'em." Bill hawked phlegm and spat into the street.

"Even asked me if I'd seen you, but of course I hadn't."

"Thanks," Alvarez said.

Cody leaned forward and peered into the darkness. "Don't mention it. Where's your pard?"

Alvarez ignored the question and took a better grip on the butt of his revolver.

The bay shifted just enough to jiggle the buggy, and the buffalo robe slipped off Cody's lap, revealing a Winchester. Cody peered down at Alvarez for a long minute, then laughed dryly. "Sorry for the weapon, but I had half a mind to shoot the good police commissioner square in his lights if he tried anything with me." He slipped the long gun into a scabbard under his seat.

Alvarez pulled his hand out of his coat pocket and blew on his fingers to warm them.

"By the way, seems Ulysses is on the loose. I got word from Maggie this afternoon."

Alvarez considered the news. "Where'd he go?"

"Hell if I know. Hill's a strange one. Maggie didn't trust him for shit and said he could be mean. I always pegged him for a slick little coward, but I've been wrong before."

"Unless I miss my guess, he'll come looking for us."

"Could be, though you've got trickier bastards than him on your trail right now."

Alvarez stamped his freezing feet. "You have any suggestion?"

Cody sniffed. "Well, I said I'd help any way I could, and I will. Still, it'll be tougher'n courting a Cheyenne virgin to get you out of town with the law on the prowl damn near everywhere. You're close to boxed in already."

"But you know a way out of the box."

Cody laughed deep in his throat. "Maybe an old fox like me knows a way out of the henhouse."

Alvarez grinned and let the old scout help him up into the buggy.

Police Commissioner Theodore Paine ground the butt of his cigar under his heel and pulled up his coat collar against the damp air seeping into his bones. He walked all the way around the depot, then walked it again. When he passed the big front entrance a second time, a porter pushing a broom over the polished terrazzo floor just inside nodded and gave him a big broad-toothed grin. Paine just scowled back.

He heard the hansom rattling over the cobblestones before he saw it, but he knew in his bones who it was; when it pulled to a stop fifteen yards from the covered boardwalk, he stepped down into the street and strode over to it and got in.

The gentleman cleared his throat and took a deep drag on his own cigar. The red glow almost but not quite illuminated his face. "Do you have the time?"

"One o'clock," Paine said. "A little after."

The gentleman sighed, as if from fatigue. "Do you have them?"

"No, sir. Not yet."

"But you will." It wasn't a question.

"We'll find them. Before the night is out."

"This was not supposed to happen, Theodore," the other man said. "You made a serious mistake trusting that cripple. You can't afford to make another."

"We'll find them," Paine repeated.

"Do I make myself clear?"

Paine choked down the gall rising in his throat. "I said we'd find them" was all he could say.

The gentleman laughed and gave Paine a little condescending pat on the knee as a father would an errant son, letting the singular insult of the gesture sink in before he spoke again. "See that you do, Theodore. See that you do."

Chapter 16

A COLD DRIZZLE WAS FALLING BY THE TIME Cody dropped Alvarez off at the tumbledown faro den where Comstock was waiting.

If they were going to get out of Denver, they'd have to do it on horseback, and Cody left them while he went to look for mounts. He knew where they might be able to lay their hands on some good horseflesh, no questions asked, he said, as long as he had a couple of hours to arrange it.

They filled the time playing cards, sipping at their whiskeys, and trying to ignore the smell of green beer, stale vomit, and too many unwashed, weatherbeaten men. No matter how much he drank, Comstock couldn't kill the pain in his leg, and Alvarez had grave concerns about his ability to sit a horse when the time came, but when he brought it up, Comstock only glared at him and changed the subject. And, in truth, they didn't have much choice but to try. When Cody returned at half past two, he told them the police were still out in force, so they finished their drinks and spent another hour winding through the wet back alleys beyond the tracks. As morning approached, the drizzle turned to rain and then sleet; Cody got lost twice but eventually found a particular dirt lane running parallel to the river, followed it for a mile, and turned west onto a path heading down to the breaks of the South Platte. The road petered out into an old wagon track turning to half-frozen mud that sucked so hard at the buggy wheels they had to pull over into a stand of cottonwoods.

"We'll walk from here," Cody said. It was almost five o'clock.

The weather had a way of leveling them. Cody strode through the muck looking more like a derelict than a famous showman: his gait was awkward because of the chronic pain in his crotch, and his shoulder-length hair was plastered down as the cold rain dripped off his high white hat.

Alvarez had his head pulled as far down into his coat as he could, but he was still freezing. "Goddamn weather," he grumbled. Comstock, limping along behind him, wiped his runny nose with the back of his hand and swore, too.

"Dammit is right," Cody said. "I could use a toilet. Still it ain't much farther."

"Better not be," Comstock said bitterly.

"I reckon you're in luck the weather turned this bad," Cody said as the raw wind snatched at his baritone. "It'll discourage those police boys from spotting you."

"Until they find our frozen carcasses," Comstock grumbled. His kidskin shoes were soaked through. "Or at least mine. Then you can go to my funeral just like old Arnold's."

"Maybe I'll do just that," Cody said sourly.

"Shit." Comstock ignored the old scout as he limped

past him. "It's starting to snow."

"For God's sake, let's just get this over with," Alvarez snapped at both of them. "If Bill says it ain't far, I'll take his word for it—for now." He hunched his shoulders to shake some of the ice water out of his coat. It felt like it weighed twenty pounds.

The ruts turned east at a grove of river willows. Cold mud oozed up around their ankles and the track disappeared altogether.

"Almost there. A quarter mile, maybe, where the river bends," Cody said, almost to himself.

But it turned out he was right. The livery was just where he said it would be, hard on the east bank of the Platte. An open corral surrounded by barbed-wire fencing ran along the bank. Three sleepy horses standing near a broken bale of hay raised their heads and broke wind at the sound of the men's boots on the icy grass, and one high-spirited animal nickered and stamped, but Bill crooned to them and they went back to sleep. The first fat snowflakes were piling up in the stiff mane hair and on their eyelashes, giving them a ghostly appearance.

The only sign of human habitation was the thin ribbon of smoke rising from a round chimney at the back of the little corrugated iron shed guarding a sorry-looking rail gate that slapped back and forth in the wind. The wind took the smoke and scattered it, but it was a cheerful sign nonetheless: someone was around the place.

"See, I told you," Cody said brightly. He knocked sharply on a warped old door with a gloved fist.

"Shit," Comstock said yet again, and Alvarez agreed with him in silence.

Someone inside was up and moving, setting up a clanging noise on the iron skin of the hut.

Alvarez reached into his coat pocket for the Smith and Wesson; the steel was so cold it almost burned his fingers.

Cody knocked again and announced himself in his best dramatic voice. The horses in the corral nickered and stamped on the freezing earth.

The door creaked open on rusty hinges, revealing a short round man in dirty underwear and torn overalls who rubbed at his eyes with one fist when he saw them. They felt a comforting rush of warm air from inside. The little man spat a stream of brown tobacco juice through the doorway past Cody, barely missing Comstock.

"That you, William?"

"It is I," Cody answered, sweeping off his hat out of old habit and dusting the short man with wet snow in the process.

"What the hell you want, William?" He brushed at the snow with fingers that left black smears on his union suit.

Comstock groaned. "I thought this was all arranged, you sonofabitch!"

Cody shot him a hard look that shut him up. "We want to come in out of the cold, for one thing, Bob. My friends here need horses and saddles, for another," he said patiently, glossing over Comstock's complaint.

The man sniffed and worked at his cud. "Well, whyn't you say so?" He opened the door wider and beckoned them inside.

The shed was surprisingly warm. A potbellied stove glowed cherry red along the back wall, and as the visitor's coats began to steam in the close air, the little man opened the stove door and tossed in three big lumps of hard coal. The furnishings were sparse. Two straight-backed chairs, a wobbly set of shelves, and a worktable stacked with papers so filthy they resembled small piles of mining slag in the dim glow of the one kerosene lamp high up on a shelf, its chimney so sooty the flame was barely visible. The place smelled of coal and kerosene, tobacco and spit.

The short man rubbed coal dust into his overalls. "Need horses, do you? Damn strange time of night to be needing horses." He gave Cody a broad idiot's grin. "What the hell you up to, Bill?"

Cody ignored the question. "Two horses, Bob," he said. "That's all we require. Two of your best. Gentle of foot, stout of heart."

Bob grinned and spat again. The hard-packed earthen floor was sticky with tobacco juice. "That's the on'y kind I got, Colonel. You know that."

Cody wagged a gloved finger and feigned a scolding tone. "Not so, Bob. Not so. I've seen you sell glue on the hoof for three times what it's worth."

Bob appeared genuinely hurt by the remark. "I never sold no glue-pots to you or your'n, Colonel, and I damn sure wouldn't now. No matter what time of night it is." He shuffled uneasily as if waiting for Bill to say something else, and at length he pointed to the two chairs. "You boys want to set a spell?"

Alvarez shook his head, but Comstock lowered himself onto one. The dry wood groaned under his weight.

Cody cleared his throat and got down to business. "Two horses, good riding saddles, a couple of feedbags of oats, and saddle blankets. That's what we require. How much?"

Bob whistled under his breath, and a dribble of tobacco juice ran down his chin. He wiped at it with the back of his hand and missed. "Tall order. Don't have the saddles. Could get 'em by noon, mebbe. A hundred-and-a-quarter each for the horses, fifty for the saddle an' robe, another five for the bridle and bit. I could throw in the oats." Bob pulled a stub of pencil out of a trouser pocket, licked the lead, and jotted down some figures on the topmost piece of paper in the stack on the desk. "Call it… oh, hell, three hundred fifty dollars flat for both."

Alvarez whistled under his breath. "That's damn steep."

Cody motioned again to keep them quiet. "What'll it cost to get it all together by sunup? Along with some canned beans, a slab of bacon, and maybe some cornbread?"

Bob scratched his head. "I ain't got the saddles, Bill. An' that grub's out of the question. It's the middle of the gol-danged night."

"How much? By sunup. Including the vittles, or we'll take our business elsewhere."

Bob spit out his whole cud and wiped at his chin while he considered. This time, he did all the necessary figuring in his head. "Twenty-five extra. Apiece. That's four hun-dred."

"I can add," Cody snapped.

Bob nodded.

"How much is my discount?"

Bob looked at his shoe. "Now, Bill, I can't do that no more." Embarrassment colored his face under the grime and he pulled a plug of chew from his hip pocket and bit off a chunk the size of a silver dollar. "I'm sorry, but you're into Mr. Gaines for more'n my whole year's wages. And that's just what I know about. He'd skin me alive if I tried to give you your old discount now." He chewed and spit and didn't look up again.

Cody shrugged and turned to Comstock and Alvarez. "I spend a lifetime building this frontier and this is what it comes down to. I can't buy two horses on account! I save the life of this man's father back in seventy-six and this is the thanks I get!" He delivered the little speech with high drama solely for Bob's benefit.

The little man laughed nervously and worked the cud around in his mouth. "Oh, hell, Bill, you never saved my old man's life. You know it and so do I." He still kept his eyes averted.

"Did so. In the very same skirmish in which I took the scalp of Yellow Hand. The first scalp for Custer!" Cody fairly shouted, but he was shouting past little Bob, as if he were trying to reach some imaginary audience beyond the tin walls. "Your daddy would've gone under with an arrow betwixt his ribs and his topknot'd be hanging from a Cheyenne coup stick this very day if it weren't for me."

It struck Alvarez that Cody actually believed it.

Bob sighed and spat. "Whatever," he said, letting the matter slide. "I still can't give you no discount, Bill. Mr. Gaines makes the rules, an' he says it's cash on the barrel head for you."

Cody's face reddened and he swore something under his breath, then stomped outside, letting the door bang shut behind him.

Bob shook his head sadly.

Alvarez followed Cody. The snow was coming down harder.

"I thought this deal was all worked out," Alvarez said, trying unsuccessfully to keep any hint of accusation out of his voice.

Cody gave him a hurt look. "Should have been, pard. I know they've got horses. I just didn't count on Bob being so damn loyal." The words caught in the old man's throat. "I got to go to the toilet," he said softly, to no one in particular.

Alvarez let him go and stepped back inside and leaned over to whisper into Comstock's ear. "How much money you got, Ben?"

Comstock grumbled something about Cody's manhood, but he checked his pockets. "A hundred. Maybe a little more thanks to them boys at the faro table."

Alvarez felt the little bulge in his money belt and did some quick calculations. He grinned at Bob, but there was more menace in it than good humor. "I've bought enough horses to know when it's time to strike a deal," he said. "It's time now."

Bob grinned stupidly back at him. He looked like he was about to wet himself. "I don't have to sell you nothing at all."

"But you will." Alvarez fished the old Smith and Wesson out of his coat pocket and stuck it into the waist-band of his trousers.

Bob gulped and eyed the piece.

"I think he's got you there, friend," Comstock said menacingly. He leaned back in the rickety old chair and folded his arms over his chest to watch the show.

Alvarez draped his hand over the butt of his weapon. "Now, then, we'll pay a hundred each for the horses and seventy-five more for both saddles and bridles and some oats. You can forget about food for us if it comes down to it. That's two-seventy-five total—if we approve of the horses, and if it's all ready by seven-thirty. That gives you something over two hours.

"That ain't much time," Bob whined.

Alvarez pulled the Smith and Wesson and spun the cylinder, checking the loads. "But we have a deal, don't we?"

Bob worked the cud hard. "The whole lot's worth three-fifty."

"Two-seventy-five. In one minute, it goes down to two-and-a-quarter."

Bob stiffened a little. It took an effort for him to pull his eyes away from the gun and meet Alvarez's gaze. "Christ, you're talkin' highway robbery."

"No," Alvarez said. "Horse trading. And the bid's about to go to two-fifty."

"Three-twenty-five," Bob said.

"Two-seventy-five."

"Three-ten's as low as I can go."

"Two-eighty-five. Two-ninety if you can find the beans and bacon. And when you write it up, say the sale price was three hundred dollars minus a discount for Buffalo Bill."

Bob inhaled a deep breath and held it. He spat, let out the breath, and spat again. "All right, I'm apt to lose my job, but two hundred ninety it is for the whole shebang. I can't promise how good the saddles'll be, though."

"Good riding is all that matters," Alvarez said expansively now that the price was set. "And no fancy cowboy getup, either. Just good leather, well broken-in. My partner here needs as soft a ride as he can get.

Bob thought for a moment. "Come to think of it, I might have something that'll work."

"I thought as much."

"Show me the money first."

"You show us the horseflesh, and we'll show you the

money."

"How do I know you won't try to steal 'em from me?"

Alvarez replied, "You don't."

Bob sighed. "You're some horse trader."

"When I have to be," Alvarez said, and he tucked the old revolver back into his pocket. He turned his attention to Comstock. "Ben, go get Bill and tell him the deal's cut. And tell him he got his discount."

The day was an hour old by the time Comstock and Alvarez got their truck wrapped in oilcloth and tied behind the old saddles cinched onto the two gelding quarterhorses Bob had found. The snow was coming faster and beginning to stick everywhere, and the river and trees were lost in the thin swirling grayness.

Bob watched from the doorway, that fat wad of greenbacks making a huge bulge in his trouser pocket. "Them's the best saddles I could find," he said, spitting a fresh brown stream into the show. "At least they been broken in good."

Cody, greatly appeased by the discount marked clearly on the bill of sale, stood by as Alvarez and Comstock swung up into the saddle. Comstock grimaced as he settled his injured leg into the stirrup, but when Alvarez asked if he was all right, he waved it off without a word.

"Them's prime horses," Bob said.

"They'll do," Alvarez offered, and he pulled his coat collar up to keep the snow off. His gelding, a sturdy big-boned black, shivered and raised its tail and dumped a pile of steaming dung into the yard.

"A good horse always shits before it goes to work," Cody said with a self-satisfied laugh.

"It's damn sure got its work cut out for it today," Alvarez allowed. "We'll see you in Pueblo, Bill?"

"I'll be there. Train leaves at four this afternoon. You got a hellatious ride, though." The old scout rubbed his gloved hands together. The wet snow piling up on his hat brim and shoulders made him look like some old graystone courthouse statue. "Ted Paine's boys'll be checking every damn road between here and Manitou Springs, you can be sure of that. My advice to you is to turn east and keep riding."

Alvarez sniffed and hunkered down deeper into his coat. "I figure we'll follow the river, then skirt along the front range. This snow'll hide our tracks. Tell Gertrude we'll be coming along."

Cody shook his head. "If she waits for you, she'll never get the old coot underground."

"Just tell her," Comstock snapped, and he dug his heels into his bay gelding's ribs, nudging it into the teeth of the storm without another word of farewell. Alvarez grinned and doffed his hat, mimicking the old scout, then nudged his black into motion as well.

Within seconds, they were lost to sight in the snow.

"Two old farts like that'll freeze to death 'fore nightfall," Bob said as he carved a new chunk of tobacco out of a plug. "Damn shame to lose the horses."

Bill sniffed and shifted his weight to ease the pressure on his bladder. "They'll make out fine. I doubt there's a storm made that could stop them boys." Then he gave Bob a hearty handshake and turned his steps back toward town, toward Louisa's apartment and the absolute certainty that Theodore Paine would be there before the morning was out with a million questions.

Chapter 17

T HE SNOW FELL THICK AND FAST. Comstock and Alvarez guided their horses past a few low adobe buildings barely visible in the storm, found the edge of the cottonwood and willow thickets lining the banks of the South Platte, and cut through the trees to the flat, frozen riverbank. Then they turned their backs to the driving north wind and hunkered down, pulled their necks into their collars and the brims of their hats down over their ears, and let the horses go. Only the sound of rattling wind and blowing horses reached their ears as they rode. Gray crusts formed on their backs, cracked and fell away, then formed again. Meltwater from their upturned collars trickled down their necks, dampening their shirts.

A half mile, a mile, then two, then four. Always onward, south along the riverbottom, pushed on by the wind and driving snow.

Comstock stopped once to relieve himself, and by the time he remounted, his saddle was coated with a thin layer of soft ice. He scraped it off with his coat sleeve, hauled himself aboard the bay, and nudged it into motion. Alvarez was fifty yards ahead by then, and he had to dig his heels into the bay's flanks to get it to quicken its pace grudgingly.

"Goddamn weather," he grumbled when he came up even with Alvarez.

Alvarez's head turned within the encircling coat collar stiff as a tortoise shell, and he looked at his companion. "You all right?"

"Why shouldn't I be?"

"I don't want you wearing out on me."

"You're the one with a bum leg."

"You're the one with buckshot holes in your butt."

Comstock grimaced and wiped snow out of his eyebrows with a gloved hand. "I guess we're even, then, old pard."

"I guess," Alvarez said.

"Crazy, ain't it?" Comstock laughed out loud. "Two crippled-up old farts out for a little ride on a beautiful autumn day, I mean."

Alvarez leaned off to one side, put a finger against one nostril, and blew.

"Makes me wish I'd stayed in El Paso and read about this whole shebang in the papers," Comstock added, but Alvarez said nothing.

"Sure as hell wish it'd quit snowing," Comstock offered after another quarter-mile.

Alvarez squirmed a little to break the snowcrust off his shoulders and snapped the reins over the black's neck. "Wishing won't make it so, Benjamin. All I know is, we've got a hard ride ahead, and I don't need to worry about a straggler."

Comstock set his heels to the bay again. "Worry about

your ownself, you sonofabitch!" he barked as the bay pulled into the lead.

Police Commissioner Theodore Paine stubbed out two-thirds of a perfectly good cigar and massaged his temples with both hands. By any reckoning, all of this business should have been settled hours ago. He looked at his pocketwatch. Three hours, actually. As soon as they'd gotten the first report that the fugitives were seen riding out of town along the river. And still he waited. Stalled. It was a weakness. Misplaced loyalty, he supposed.

A man could die from misplaced loyalty.

He slipped his watch back into his left vest pocket and opened the drawer in front of him. It was empty except for the Colt Peacemaker and a double-barreled derringer and two boxes of shells. He loaded the weapons carefully, stuck the derringer into his right vest pocket, laid the Colt and the box of shells on the desktop, and closed the drawer. His holster hung empty on the coat tree by the door, but he hesitated to fetch it. Something about strapping on the gun would mean no turning back now; once the manhunt began, he couldn't back away from any of it. Not that he'd ever had a real opportunity or inclination to do so. Old debts were always troublesome because you never knew when they were going to come due, but a debt was a debt nevertheless: when it was time to pay, you paid.

He fetched the holster. The belt held thirty extra bullets and the gun—a heavy weight to carry on a hip unused to it. He pushed the cartridges into the little leather loops and slid the Colt into the oiled leather.

"Shit," he said to himself as he strapped it on. The weight of the gun was nothing compared to the weight on his conscience. *When it was time to pay, you paid.*

Someone knocked on his office door.

"Come in."

A young constable stuck his head inside. "Excuse me, sir. The ordnance you requested is ready."

"Thank you, Henry."

"You're welcome, sir. Is that all?"

"Please make sure you send that telegram to Pueblo so they'll know I'll be out of touch for at least a day."

"Yes, sir. Anything else?"

Paine shook his head, and the constable withdrew.

Two rifles and a shotgun requisitioned from the armory along with enough ammunition to blast half the population of Colorado to kingdom come waited at the front desk, his to use however he wished for nothing more than his signature.

And all because of two old men who should have kept their noses out of it.

Except that he was the one who'd ordered them to get their noses into it in the first place.

Well, the holster *was* heavy, but it was comfortable in a worn, familiar way. This weapon had been his favorite side-arm back in Leavenworth days; he'd been able to shoot the head off a squirrel at fifty paces with it, a demonstration that'd had a remarkably quieting effect on the rowdier prisoners. So powerful was the effect, in fact, that he'd only had to draw on three men in all his time there. Just three, and all promptly buried in the prison potter's field. He'd used the Colt more often to crack skulls than to shoot with.

The trouble was, he'd used the butt end of the weapon on more than just the prisoners, which was what had gotten him into trouble with the Army. The Fort Leavenworth commander hadn't taken kindly to having one of his subalterns pistol-whipped by a lowly prison guard in an argument over a woman, and he'd demanded the warden discharge the guard forthwith. Ted Paine had been stripped of his job and driven off the post within the hour.

The Denver police, to their credit, hadn't held that little skirmish against him; a bright young man with a knack for cracking heads came in handy around the gambling dens and rough saloons. Rotgut whiskey and gold dust from the mountain diggings were an explosive combination in those days, and Constable Ted Paine had been very good at defusing trouble. And he'd used another hard lesson of the Leavenworth experience to good effect as well: he'd made it a point to curry favor with the powerful.

When the Democratic ward bosses came around asking favors, he always made sure he was ready to do their bidding. Whether it was hauling drunks to the polls so they could cast a bogus vote or arresting miners suspected of Republican leanings on trumped-up vagrancy charges or standing aside when a contrary shopkeeper's store was ransacked, Officer Paine had done his best always to help the men who wielded the power and handed out the patronage. He'd come to the attention of the party's state-wide leadership quickly, and in short order he'd found himself with a comfortable inside job watching out for the interests of highly placed politicians and their cronies.

It hadn't taken much brainpower to parlay that sort of duty into money and position in turn-of-the-century Denver, and Ted Paine had brains if he had anything.

He opened his humidor and put a half dozen cigars into his inner coat pocket for later smoking, then locked his desk and turned down the gas jets. A false twilight descended on the room immediately; it was only mid-afternoon, but the snow was blowing so thick and hard it might as well have been dusk.

Maybe he was too smart for his own good, he thought ruefully. The good life always extracted a price, usually when it was least expected. Now he had this nasty business to attend to because he'd allowed something to get out of hand. And even though he had no particular stomach for it, no one else could be trusted to do it. You danced to the tune the fiddler played.

Not that he cared a whit about what had happened to Arnold Toothacker: the old man was a drunkard and an embarrassment, and his death was no loss to society. But he respected Tom Alvarez. More than that, he considered him a dangerous foe even if he was a crippled-up old man, and when he got down to the bottom of it, it was that danger that was making him procrastinate now.

He stepped out of his office and into the long corridor. He could see the guns leaning against the wall just inside the rail that separated the public waiting area from the offices. Paine strode quickly down the corridor, the sound of his boots ringing off the cold plastered walls, the Colt slapping at his thigh with each step.

The desk sergeant saw him and gave him a little salute. "It's all here, sir," the sergeant said.

"Then let's get it loaded. Daylight doesn't last long enough as it is."

Ulysses Hill stood in the shelter of the alleyway across the street from the Denver Police Headquarters for a very long time, watching the constables come and go. The snow settled out of the gusting eddies and drifted down slowly, piling up around his feet. He was freezing; every few minutes he stomped his feet and rubbed his hands together to keep the blood moving.

A police wagon rolled up in front of the station and stopped. The pair of gray Percherons pulling it looked like gigantic hunched ghosts as they steamed in the wet half-light.

He stomped and waited, reached into his trouser pocket and wrapped his hand around his little gun. It was a completely inadequate weapon except where it could be used by surprise, and surprise here was out of the question. He would have to find another way to get even with them for the way they'd preyed on him, making him use his own greed against himself until he'd destroyed his own comfortable life.

Perhaps he'd go to Pueblo; that was where the newspapers said the commissioner was going for the old marshal's funeral.

Hill smiled grimly at the irony. Pueblo was the place. They wouldn't be looking for him there.

The station house door opened, and a tall man in a brown tweed overcoat with a rifle in each hand hurried down the icy steps. A constable toting a shotgun and a wooden ammunition box followed. The man in tweed handed the rifles up to someone in the wagon, accepted the shotgun from the constable, and took a hand up into the wagon himself. The constable made two more trips into the station for the rest of the weaponry.

As soon as the last of the armament was loaded aboard the wagon, the Percherons lowered their heads and leaned into the traces.

Hill jammed his hands deeper into his pockets for

warmth and slipped out of the alley and began following the wagon on foot through the snow and gloom. It would soon lose him, but that hardly mattered. His shoes slipped in the freezing slush, and the full force of the wind stung his eyes and ears, but no one saw him. The very act of moving warmed him, giving him strength for the task that lay ahead.

Tom Alvarez called a halt before what little daylight the afternoon afforded faded away altogether. The wind had let up considerably, and the snow was falling only intermittently. They'd come upon a grassy meadow in the shelter of a willow thicket running down to the river's edge. Drifts two and three feet deep had piled up in some places, but the snow was only six inches deep in the lee of the thicket where the willows had broken the wind's back, and in the heart of the woods there were places where the autumn leaf litter was bare of snow, giving the horses some forage. They couldn't hope for more.

Comstock searched through the deadfall timber for what firewood he could find while Alvarez hobbled the horses and scouted out the driest spot to make camp. He considered a cold camp but gave up on the idea because they'd need the strength a hot meal would give them. And, thanks to Bill Cody and his liveryman friend, they had decent field rations: bacon and canned peaches—both now frozen—some two-day-old cornbread, and a paper packet of parched and ground coffee. If they could find enough dry wood to get a fire going, they'd have a meal that, under the circumstances, would be as good as a feast.

In a half hour they had a fire going and the bacon thawing and snow melting in the coffeepot. By the time full night fell, just the smell of cooking meat and hot coffee had cheered them more than they would have thought possible—or would have admitted to each other. They ate ravenously, then spread out their ground cloths and saddle blankets over piles of leaves for passable beds.

"Why the hell did we do this, anyway, Tom?" Comstock asked as he poured himself a second cup of coffee. He fished half a peach out of the icy syrup with his pocketknife and passed the tin to Alvarez.

Tom drank off some of the syrup and gobbled down a peach whole. The sweetness cut the greasy, wet-wood taste of the slab of bacon. "It beats staying in Denver and getting assassinated in our sleep," he said seriously, smacking his lips.

Comstock groaned and turned his sore backside to the fire. "You ain't wrong there."

Alvarez stretched his bad leg out toward the fire. "You all right?"

"Stiff as a board. Otherwise, I'll live."

"You sure?"

Comstock grunted. "You let me worry about me."

"Fine." Alvarez slipped another piece of deadfall wood into the fire. It popped, sending a shower of orange sparks swirling skyward.

Comstock finished his coffee, chewing the last bitter grounds carefully to get all the good out of them, then he leaned back and rested his head on his saddle. "It's going to be harder going tomorrow than today."

"Couldn't be."

"Will be. Look there." He pointed overhead. Stars blinked on and off as a thin veil of cloud streamed by. "The wind's shifted. This early in the season, this'll all melt faster'n it came down today, and these bottoms'll be muddier'n shit. We'll have to go to higher ground."

"Where someone following us will have a better chance of finding us."

"That's right."

"Goddamn Colorado weather," Alvarez said with a sigh. Still, he felt a little thrill of excitement quicken his blood. His bad leg ached deep inside the bone, but it was like an old friend: irritating, tiresome, and a comfort at the same time. Bad snowmelt coffee, half-cooked bacon, frozen peaches, sleeping on wet ground on a night that would stay below freezing, and an aching limb were like a strange tonic, sweeping away the lethargy that had crept over him so slowly over the recent years he hadn't even been aware it was there, sapping his strength, strangling him in his own inaction. "I'll have one more cup of that godawful coffee of yours, Benjamin," he said, and he yawned. "Then you take the first watch, and be damn sure you keep the fire going. I don't want my ass froze to the ground when I wake up!"

Comstock gave him a wicked grin that couldn't quite mask the grimace of pain.

It was well past dark and the clouds were gone, leaving the cold blue stars in their wake, before the police wagon broke through the last big drift and the Percherons struggled up the final hundred yards to the log hunting lodge overlooking the gorge of the South Platte. Welcoming smoke curled from the lodge chimney, and two men in buffalo-robe coats greeted the constables and helped un-hitch the gray horses and get them into a lean-to, where plenty of dry straw and oats and cracked corn awaited. The smaller man showed the travelers into the lodge and poured a round of good bourbon whiskey.

"How soon you want to leave in the morning?" the small man named Dan asked as soon as the drinks were poured. He grinned as he spoke, showing jagged, blackened teeth.

Ted Paine lifted the tumbler of whiskey to his lips and took a long, burning, satisfying sip. He was dead tired, but it was a good tired—coming from fatigue born of action. He'd been sitting at a desk too long. "Early morning. First light. On rested horses."

The small man nodded. He took a plug of tobacco from a coat pocket and shaved off a hunk with a hunting knife. "The men you're after. Outlaws?"

Paine shrugged. "Wanted on suspicion of theft."

"Don't seem like much to go manhuntin' over."

"That's my concern, not yours." He lit a cigar and purposely didn't offer the little man one.

An odd half-grin played across Dan's ugly face. "You sure they come this way?"

"They'll be going south, toward Pueblo, if my hunch is right. To bury a friend of theirs."

"What'll you do when we catch 'em?"

Pained looked over his shoulder at the two rifles and the shotgun resting against the wall. "You know how to use weapons like that?"

The big man chuckled easily and raised his glass in a silent toast to Ted Paine and the thrill of the hunt.

Tom Alvarez rubbed his bad leg to get the blood going below the knee. He was so cold every part of his body ached, the leg worst of all. He'd seen gangrenous limbs swollen black from frostbite and ready for the surgeon's saw, and the prospect of this happening to him made him think more about his own mortality than he cared to.

Ben Comstock stirred the puny fire with a green willow stick. He looked as gray as the dead wet ashes on the edges of the fire.

"How you feeling, Ben?"

"Fine as frog's hair," Comstock said softly. "Can't get the damn fire goin'."

"Sure could use a crackling fire to take the cold out of my bones."

Comstock cast an eye to the sky. "You'll warm up enough later. Right now, I'd just like to get the coffee het up."

A chunk of packed snow fell from the top branches of the nearest willow and thudded on the ground, narrowly missing the fire. "Better give me some coffee before some damn snowball puts the fire out altogether." Alvarez drank and rubbed some more and struggled to his feet, then hobbled across the little meadow to check on the horses, found they'd survived the night no worse for wear, and went back to the fire. His toes were beginning to burn, but it was a pain he welcomed: he had the circulation going again. Comstock hadn't moved.

"If it's going to warm up today, I'd just as soon it got to it," Alvarez grumbled.

Comstock swore under his breath. "The horses are footsore. Maybe we ought to give 'em a rest."

"They can rest when we get to Manitou Springs, maybe. We can try for a train there." Pueblo seemed an impossibly long way off.

Comstock sniffed and started to say something, but changed his mind. He passed the coffee and started to get up, the exertion was too much for him, and he grunted and sank back to his knees. His face was shiny with sweat.

Alvarez squinted at him and whistled softly. "You got an infection, don't you?"

"I hurt some," Comstock admitted.

"Give me a look."

"Go to hell."

"You can't ride that way."

"The horses are tired anyway."

"The horses are fine. It's you that's worn out." Alvarez put some more wood on the fire, banking it carefully against the glowing coals, and chewed over this new turn of events. If he left Comstock and pressed on, at least one of them would stand a chance of facing down Arnold's killers, but he had no stomach at all for leaving a friend to die, and alone, Comstock would surely die—one way or the other.

Alvarez tried to remember what he could about field surgery. It wasn't much; he'd never done much more than splinting broken bones or lancing boils in his life. Still, he had a good pocketknife, and the fire was beginning to burn bright. If Ben's wounds were full of pus, it might just be possible to lance and drain them before the infection went too deep.

"Give me a look, Ben," he ordered.

"I said go to hell." But there was resignation in the way Comstock said it, and after a moment's hesitation, he lay back on his blanket and closed his eyes.

"God damn you to hell for slowing me up," Alvarez said gently, and he pulled out his pocketknife, opened it up, and laid the tip of the blade against a glowing red coal.

Ted Paine stood in the stirrups and swung his binoculars through one hundred eighty degrees of arc from the dark strip of the South Platte to the white upthrust of Pike's Peak to the south to the brilliant whiteness of the eastern horizon. The sun blazed off the frozen plain as endless as pack ice at sea. He twisted in the saddle and waved at the police van far in the rear. The Percherons and the narrow-wheeled wagon were bogged down in the muck, and the driver waved back in a simple circular motion that couldn't be misunderstood. The wagon would have to turn around and return to the hunting lodge. From now on, all tracking would have to be done on horseback.

Paine turned his back to the van. "Is there a better place to get a look at the terrain than this?"

The smaller of the two contract hunters spat a wad of tobacco into a rapidly melting snowbank. It left a small brown hole in the drift. The other hunter sat silently on a sturdy gelding, cradling his long gun in his arms. "This is the best there is," Dan said. "We're on the main road south, and it's the highest elevation this side of the front range. What you think, Harve?"

The big man shrugged and hunkered down in his buffalo coat.

Pained scanned the horizon with his binoculars one more time. "Might they follow the river?"

"Could be, but it'd be risky business. The ice'll go out in a hurry in this weather. 'Sides, the gorge deepens right quick and them old men don't know their way from what you tell me."

"A little risk won't stop them." He paused, concentrating on a little strip of the river. Something was moving far off, where the Platte emptied out of the foothills. Was it smoke, the shimmer of warming air coming off the snow, or just his imagination? He kept looking.

"You think we ought to go that way?"

"I think if I was them, that's the way I'd be going," Paine said. "How long before my men can get back here with their mounts?"

The little man considered the question. "Hour. Mebbe more."

Paine glanced over his shoulder. The Percherons were wheeling around, pulling the van out of the mire with agonizing slowness. "We don't have time like that to waste."

The bigger of the two hunters seemed to come awake. "We don't have to wait fer 'em. Ain't nobody me an' Little Dan can't run to ground," he said.

The three of them snapped the reins over their horses' ears and they trotted forward, riding abreast. Paine nodded in the direction of the river, and they veered toward it, leaving the road behind.

Alvarez brought in the horses and rubbed them down while Comstock rested. They had to get going, and soon. The warming sun was already setting the river ice to booming, and Alvarez half expected unwelcome company at any moment.

The little piece of field surgery had gone well enough under the circumstances. Three separate wounds on Comstock's leg and left buttock had been red-hot with pus, and as soon as Alvarez touched them with the razor-sharp knife blade, they'd split open like rotten fruit. Ben had bit clear through a wad of horse blanket while Alvarez was doing the cutting but had never uttered a sound. Once he'd cauterized the wounds as well as he could, Alvarez packed snow around the leg to stanch the bleeding and wrapped it in a torn piece of his own shirttail, the only decent clean cloth at hand. Just how Comstock was going to sit a saddle all day was an open question, but Alvarez took the time with the horses to give it some thought.

His earlier optimism about the animals had been ill-founded. Sore-footed and sluggish, they stood head-down and blowing as if they'd had a stiff run, their wet hides twitching as he rubbed the wet blankets over their backs. The big black turned its head once and took a half-hearted nip at Alvarez's hip, but even its spirit seemed broken.

Alvarez found himself wishing they'd bought good Indian ponies, the kind that had the brains and the breeding to forage for themselves in wet weather. But then, ponies wouldn't have been able to carry two big men through the snowdrifts, either. Maybe what he really needed were a couple of good, strong mules. Mules were the only utterly dependable mounts a man could find these days. It was a sad state of affairs. He finished cinching the saddled and rigged up a little sling with another piece of torn cloth that would keep Comstock's leg from chafing on the worn leather fender. Then he went back to look after Comstock. There wasn't much else he could think to do.

"We'll have to keep to the high ground as much as we can," he said. "Where we can see if anyone's following." He tried hard to remember what he could about Colorado geography. "The Springs are still thirty-odd miles as the crow flies." Under the best of circumstances, that meant a full day of good, hard riding, and Comstock's newly lanced wounds would hardly make the best of circumstances.

Comstock sat facing what was left of the fire with his foot propped against a deadfall log. "That's a long way."

"You got any better ideas?"

"Can't say as I do," he said simply. He moved the leg

experimentally. "I can stand it," he said through gritted teeth.

"Maybe you shouldn't move."

"I'll live."

Alvarez looked hard at Comstock, then checked the sun. "Well, maybe we better get going, then. I'll give you a hand."

"I ain't never needed help sitting a horse before," Comstock groused, "and I reckon I don't now." He pushed the deadfall log away and struggled to his feet, steadying himself as he studied the distance separating him from the bay. "'Course, if you was to bring that rascal to me, I'd be obliged." He managed a sheepish grin.

It took several tries, but working together, they hoisted Comstock into the saddle and slipped the sling around the injured leg and secured it to the saddle horn. Then Alvarez threw his own bad leg over the saddle, endured the few seconds of nagging pain from his ancient wounds, and nudged the black in the ribs. It snorted and tossed its head, but on the second nudge, it headed up the slope away from the willow thicket and out of the gorge of the South Platte.

Chapter 18

GERTRUDE TOOTHACKER POURED the strong black coffee from her silver coffee urn into the china demitasse and handed it carefully to the big man seated across from her. He took the tiny cup in his thick-fingered hands and sipped at it appreciatively. She gave him a polite smile and purposely kept her eyes averted from the snowmelt running off his boots and collecting in a puddle on her waxed hardwood floor; she was too much a gentlewoman to worry about a wet floor when this friend of her husband's had made the effort to pay her a visit.

"I'm glad you stopped by, Marshal Tilghman. It would have meant a great deal to Arnold." Her tone was as formal as the words themselves, and she knew he couldn't tell how difficult it was even to mention her husband's name to this man, the first of his old friends to come calling on the grieving widow.

"He was a good man," Bill Tilghman said, and he started to say something more but couldn't find the right words and took another sip of the coffee to fill the silence.

She poured herself a little coffee and carried the cup and saucer to her parlor window. A fine lacework of ice crystals etched the glass in leaf-shaped patterns, but the snow in the yard was already going. The black holes Tilghman's boots had punched in the drifts were softening at the edges already.

"Was the travel hard?" She didn't really care whether he answered. She hated winters—always had—and the sudden onslaught of yesterday's hard weather so early in the season had seemed an ill omen. It was as if, even in death, Arnold were finding a new way to burden her. She had met the coffin at the train station in the middle of the night, supervised the transfer of his body to the undertaker's, and come home for a few hours of sleep only to be awakened by the rattling of the shutters and the moaning wind coming in around her windows and down the chimney.

By midmorning, the show had sealed her indoors and her home was no longer her refuge and her strength, but her prison. She'd coped with Arnold's death admirably until then, but the early snowstorm had made her feel vulnerable, alone, and angry. She had been living for years with the possibility of Arnold's death, first because he was in such a dangerous occupation, then later because he drank so heavily, but when it actually came—especially so brutally— she found herself utterly unprepared. She'd cried yesterday morning for the first time since the news had come, and she'd screamed into the teeth of the storm, cursing Arnold for leaving her, cursing God for taking him, and finally cursing herself for her weakness. She'd cried through the night, and only after dawn, when she'd cried herself out, did she collect herself, put the coffee on to boil, and sit down to wait, but for what, she didn't know.

It turned out to be Bill Tilghman.

"The morning train was late yesterday or I would've been by earlier," Tilghman was saying mostly to make small talk to fill the void. He spoke soothingly out of consideration for the circumstances, his Oklahoma accent softening it even more. "I only knew your husband on the cusp, you might say. Run into him out along the Cimarron a time or two. He was an honest man. There ain't enough like him nowadays, I can tell you that." He stared at his boots without seeming to notice the meltwater.

"Well, it was nice of you to come," she said flatly, knowing some response to so gracious a statement was necessary. The little filigree of frost on the window shrank by an eighth of an inch as she watched.

"We'll all be here for the services, the good Lord willin'." The demitasse rattled as he set it down on the low table. "A whole bunch of the boys are here already."

She nodded. "I know. Bill Cody sent me a telegram that was the floweriest thing you ever saw in your life, asking me if the pallbearers he'd selected were all right. He said he was with Arnold on the night he died. Is that true?"

Tilghman cleared his throat and studied his fingernails out of embarrassment. "I can't say that's exactly true. Arnold was with Ben Comstock. You remember Ben?"

"I know Ben," she said. "Is he coming down for the funeral?" She pressed an index finger on the leaf-shaped bit of frost and felt the little ridges turn to water. "Arnold thought a lot of him."

"That's more or less what I come to tell you." He cleared his throat again. "Well, not quite all. 'Fore I left Denver, I saw ol' Bill Cody. He says he wants you to know that Ben and Tom Alvarez are on their way here to pay their last respects, but you're not supposed to tell anyone. At least not the law." He seemed to have some trouble getting the last part out.

She turned away from the window. "I don't understand."

Tilghman rose slowly and faced her. He took his high-crowned white hat in his hands and twisted it slowly, nervously working the wet felt. "This ain't very pleasant, but I think you ought to know something. Before Arnold died he was somehow mixed up in another murder. Accordin' to Cody, Tom Alvarez reckons your husband was killed because of something he knew about that murder, and now Alvarez and Ben Comstock are on the run. I know it don't make much sense. There's only a few of us old-timers who know the story, and I ain't sure we know the whole of it."

She started to say something, but her voice cracked and she pulled a hanky out of a sleeve and blew her nose daintily, taking the time she needed to compose herself. "Mr. Tilghman, please sit down and tell me everything from the beginning." As if to encourage him, she picked up his coffee cup, poured a refill, and held it out to him.

"It ain't very pleasant," he said. He put his hat down but didn't reach for the cup.

"Life with Arnold was not very pleasant, as I'm sure you've gathered, but it was all I had." She let her voice trail off, and a deep sob broke from her in spite of her determination to keep it bottled up. The thing she dreaded facing was staring her straight in the eye, leaving her nowhere to run. Perhaps the answers would bring her a measure of peace. "Let's just say I'm a lawman's widow," she whispered, then repeated it so he could hear. The rest of what she said came out clear and strong, and with pride. "I have to know the truth about why he died. So, Marshal Tilghman, why don't you tell me everything you do know, and from the beginning, please."

The saloon was packed with gawkers by the time Bill Tilghman got there. Wyatt Earp was tossing down a free whiskey while he finished retelling his version of Doc Holliday's final days in Colorado for the local newspaperman supplying the liquor, and Bat Masterson was busy demonstrating card tricks for a young dandy at the bar. Tilghman draped his coat over a chair in the back and sat down alongside big John Poe.

Poe poured a whiskey. "How'd it go?"

Tilghman shrugged.

"She know about the murdered gal?"

"She does now."

Poe whistled softly through his teeth and shifted his tall frame uneasily. "Nasty business," he said.

Bat Masterson left the deck of cards on the bar and joined them, squeezing into a chair. "What's the widow plan to do?" He folded his manicured hands over the substantial belly falling over his glove-tanned dress belt.

"She's putting off the burial until Thursday."

"Why?"

"She wants to wait for Comstock and Alvarez."

"They may never get here."

"She knows. But she wants to give them a chance to get here if they can."

"What do you think?" Masterson fumbled in his vest pocket and came up with a silver case from which he extracted a smoke.

Tilghman eyed him. "About what?"

"Alvarez and Comstock. Why does the law want 'em?"

"Cody claims it's something personal between them and that police commissioner."

Masterson laughed. "Cody's a highly irregular source, at best." He lit his cigar and let the smoke curl around his head.

John Poe bolted the rest of his drink. "I won't argue your opinion of Cody, but I've known Ben Comstock for twenty-five years. I've never known him to deal any man a crooked hand. If he's in a fix, I'll try to help him out."

"Same goes for me with Alvarez," Tilghman said.

Masterson thought about it for a moment. "I admire your loyalty. Damned little of it around these days." Then he chuckled and passed around his hand-tooled cigar case.

Chapter 19

THE GELDINGS PLODDED SOUTHWARD over the rough terrain hugging the foot of the Ramparts. Alvarez scanned the horizon repeatedly with scratchy eyes that felt as if they were filled with dry sand, but saw nothing. Too much of this and he'd be snowblind. His head throbbed, and each step the gelding made registered a pain deep inside his leg.

He pulled his hat low, but the fierce sun blazing off the melting snow seemed to pierce his closed lids anyway, stabbing his eyes with brilliant red needles. Remembering an old trail trick, he dismounted and scooped up a handful of snow and rubbed it into his sockets. The cold drew out some of the pain, but the remedy was only temporary. He remounted and spurred his horse on. Thank God sunset came early in the high country.

At least he was better off than Comstock, who rode alongside, suffering his own torments. His head bobbed on his chest as he dozed in the saddle. Alvarez could tell he was still in the clutches of the fever, and when Alvarez asked him whether the sling was working, he got no answer.

Not that all their luck was bad. The black and the bay were making decent time picking their way around the drifts and keeping on a generally southerly course away from the river valley. The most important thing now was just to make good time. Put the miles behind them and hope for bed rest and a decent meal somewhere down the line, perhaps in Manitou Springs. They'd figure out how to get to Pueblo when the time came.

So Alvarez shielded his eyes from the blazing sun when he could and let the black horse find its own way. Patience had never been one of his virtues, but endurance had. Now he needed a large measure of both.

He called a halt at midafternoon to rest their animals. It was a chore just getting Comstock out of the saddle, and Alvarez fixed a little meal of leftover bacon and some crumbs of cornbread. He ached for a cup of good, strong coffee, but decided against taking the time to build a fire. A faint breeze from the southwest brought him the smell of pines and clean air and wet earth, and if he was very still, he could hear the trickle of snowmelt in the little arroyos running out of the front range hills and down to the nameless coulees of the high plains.

Comstock stretched out awkwardly on a patch of bare ground. "How much father you figure we have?" He rolled onto his side to get the weight off his wounds.

"Don't know," Alvarez said. "Not far now. Fifteen miles to Manitou, maybe less. I can't tell how far we've come." He reckoned it wasn't as far as he hoped. Still, the towering white monolith of Pike's Peak loomed huge on the horizon now, much closer than it had been.

"How much farther after that?"

"Can't say exactly. Pueblo's another fifty, sixty miles, ain't it?"

Comstock groaned. "That's two days' hard riding."

Alvarez lowered his gaze and scowled at his friend. Comstock was bright-eyed with the fever. "Don't worry about that. I figure we'll hop a freight in the Springs."

Comstock nodded and coughed.

"Most important thing is to get you to a sawbones," Alvarez said.

"I'm all right."

Alvarez took a step toward him and opened his mouth to argue, but the words caught in his throat. Something almost invisible, but not quite, moved at the edge of his peripheral vision. Or he thought it did. He rubbed his aching eyes.

Comstock caught the fleeting look of concern on Alvarez's face. "What is it?"

"I don't know." He rubbed again and peered into the shimmering white distance.

There it was again. Movement. Something to their northeast.

And then they both heard it—the small, soft thud in half-frozen earth, and a second later the report of a hunting rifle, coming crisp and clean over the rolling plain.

"Sonofabitch!" Comstock shouted. "You see 'em?" He tried to scramble to his feet, fell down, and tried again, this time with more success.

Alvarez strained for a look at the threat. Another bullet whizzed by with an angry hornet buzz, followed closely by the crack of the shot.

"Let's get the hell out of here!"

He caught the bay and pushed Comstock into the

saddle, then grabbed the black's reins and hauled himself aboard. As he swung his leg up, a bullet creased the horse's rump, singeing hair and drawing a bead of blood. The black let out a whine and leaped to a full gallop with Alvarez still half out of the saddle.

Comstock's bay was right behind.

"Where to?" Ben shouted as they wrestled their mounts under control and swung around, heading for the cover of the nearest high ground up a steep cut in the granite and toward the jumbled rock-and-pine fringes of the front range.

Alvarez leaned into the flying black mane to give himself as low a profile as possible. "Hell if I know!" He fumbled for the Smith and Wesson, nearly lost it, got a better grip on it, and pulled it free.

"There's some rocks west a piece." Comstock pointed the way. The bay, already winded, started to let up, but he raked its ribs with his heel.

Twisting in the saddle, Alvarez found their attackers against the snowy background and took aim. The short gun would be useless at this distance from horseback, but he squeezed off a round anyway. Maybe the old gun's booming report would carry back across the snow and grass to the ones who followed.

A bullet ripped off Comstock's hat, and a ricochet off a granite boulder sprayed chips of broken rock into Alvarez's face, bloodying him but doing no real harm.

"Whooeee!" Comstock shouted, but Alvarez couldn't tell whether it was in panic or exhilaration.

The running skirmish kept up almost as long as the light lasted, the two old men on winded horses managing somehow to stay ahead of the three well-mounted trackers. They found just enough cover to help reduce the explosive advantage of Paine's long guns, and the black and the bay stretched themselves out at the urging of the men, finding a second wind just when it was most needed. Comstock's bay led the way into the broken rocks atop the first low ridge, then they scrambled from rock to rock down the far side and up another steeper rise where the scrub timber thickened to the beginnings of real forest.

"I want to kill that bastard!" Comstock wheezed when they reached the edge of the thick timber and slowed to give the horses a breather. The slope fell away sharply; Paine and his men were visible four hundred yards downslope picking their way carefully among the rocks, saving their own horses.

Alvarez eyed Comstock closely. The run had brought fresh color to his cheeks, and the brightness in his eyes seemed to be from excitement rather than fever. The injuries didn't appear to be bothering him at all.

The thrill of the chase, Alvarez thought. Or maybe the threat of sudden death just put any other injury into perspective.

He turned his attention to the trackers. They were afoot, leading their mounts carefully, deliberately. Getting into position. One of the trackers raised a rifle and squeezed off a shot aimed right for him. He ducked and jerked the black around sideways from instinct and felt the hot concussion of the shot as it zipped past.

"That's too damn close!" He stabbed the black in the ribs, pushing it farther up the slope and into the trees, leaving Comstock to follow.

"You know where you're going?" Comstock shouted as

he got the bay moving.

Alvarez looked over his shoulder. "Nope," he said.

"Shit."

Two hundred yard farther upslope, the ridge leveled out and they crashed on through the trees into the heart of the stand. It was already twilight in the thick timber, and when the bay stepped too close to an old ponderosa, a low limb struck Comstock squarely in the chest. Sheering off with a loud crack, the limb swept him out of the saddle, and he fell hard, landing with a thud on his rump.

Alvarez wheeled the black around. "Sonofabitch! You all right?"

Comstock rolled onto his side and pulled himself slowly to his knees.

"You all right, Ben?"

Comstock gasped for air. "Wind. Got the wind knocked out is all." He struggled for breath and reached around and felt his buttocks through his trousers. "I ain't shot, if that's what you mean. Busted open some stitches, though," he moaned. He tried to get to his feet but couldn't manage it. "Lucky as hell I didn't have my leg in that damn sling of yours or I'd of busted it plumb off."

"Lucky," Alvarez agreed. He peered back toward the edge of the woods. It was impossible to tell whether their pursuers had followed them into the trees. He rested the Smith and Wesson across the saddlehorn. "Can you ride?"

Comstock stuffed his hand into the back of his trousers and brought it out smeared with fresh blood. He held the hand up to show Alvarez and wiped his fingers on his shirt. "How's this for a defensive position? You ask me, this is as good a place as any to fight the bastards."

Alvarez considered it. The cover was good, and Comstock was too beat up to ride. Much more and he wouldn't be able to fight. Just then he saw some movement, a shadow crossing a line of tall trees. He patted the black's neck to keep it quiet and cocked the revolver. "I reckon this'll do," he said.

Comstock struggled to his feet and leaned heavily against the trunk of a huge ponderosa to catch his breath, then drew and cocked his own piece. "Sure wish we had some long guns."

Alvarez dismounted, tied and hobbled both horses, and crouched behind a decaying pine trunk, all while trying to catch another glimpse of movement. "They've split up, I think."

"Makes sense."

They waited, scarcely breathing. Thirty seconds. A minute. Then three.

Comstock eased himself into a crouch and they waited some more.

The high whine of a Winchester and the simultaneous rattle of a bullet shattering the softwood of a ponderosa branch broke the stillness.

In less than a heartbeat, Tom Alvarez searched out the source of the shot, found the flicker of sunlight glinting off a blued barrel, aimed, and pulled the trigger. The Smith and Wesson bucked in his hands, and the thundering report from the old gun reverberated through the trees. He had it leveled and ready to fire again before the cloud of gunsmoke had drifted away.

Another rifle shot followed almost immediately, this time from a different direction. Comstock saw the muzzle flash and squeezed off his own round. Someone yelped with surprise and pain.

"Got one of the bastards!" Comstock said between clenched teeth. "Some shootin', huh?"

"You couldn't have hurt him bad at this range." Alvarez drew a beat on the spot where the first shot had come from. His heart was beating wildly in a surge of pure energy he hadn't felt in years, and the acrid smell of burnt powder brought back a flood of strangely pleasant memories. "Let's just hope you winged his shooting hand."

Comstock laughed. "Shootin' hand, nothing. I hope the damn bullet hit him in his manhood!"

Minutes passed. Comstock shifted his position to relieve the strain on his wounds. For what seemed like a very long time, the stillness was broken only by the excited chatter of jays settling in to roost in the trees and the far-off warning caw of a crow. Then, at last, they heard the shuffling of horses and the crunch of twigs and dry pine needles underfoot, then nothing.

Still, they waited. The twilight deepened in the woods. Although they couldn't see it, they knew the westering sun was sinking into the high peaks.

Twenty minutes later, Ted Paine shouted at them, his voice coming clear and strong through the thick woods. He was damned close.

"Give up now and we won't do any more shooting!"

Alvarez swung the Smith and Wesson in the general direction of Paine's voice. "Go straight to hell!" He pulled back the hammer and fired.

"Suit yourself!" Paine answered, and this time two rifles blazed away from different vantage points. One shot went wild, but the other smacked solidly into the rotten tree trunk less than two feet from Ben Comstock's head, showering him with pulpwood. Their horses bucked and pulled at their tethers.

Comstock glared at Alvarez and lowered his voice to a hate-filled rasp. "You better move the horses back, Thomas. Meantime, I'm goin' to kill me that bastard. I'm goin' to kill him deader'n hell! You better believe I will."

Alvarez felt the hooded eyes boring into him, could see the white teeth grinning in the gloom, and he had to look away. "I believe you will." Then he calmly emptied his pockets of the spare ammunition and went about moving the horses to a more sheltered location.

The siege was beginning.

Chapter 20

THE SINGLE KEROSENE LANTERN SWAYED back and forth above the potbellied stove, its little pool of yellow light inscribing a soft circle on the walls and plank flooring and worn seats as the train rumbled down the track at fifty miles an hour. Several of the passengers snored loudly in their seats while others huddled around the stove and tried to play a game of pitch in spite of the jostling of the night coach; still others stared out their windows at the black emptiness of the high plains.

One passenger leaned his head against the window, feeling both the cool bite of frost on the pane and the clacking hum of the wheels. A brown slouch hat pulled down low hid his features from the prying eyes of the conductor, who made it a point to walk through the car every few minutes just to keep watch on the passenger. The conductor had given him a seat at the back of the coach as far away from the lantern and the warmth of the stove as he could; he'd spent too many years riding the rails not to recognize trouble when he saw it.

But the passenger was determined to cause no trouble. Not now, anyway. Not even when the raucous, whiskey-soaked chatter of the card players nagged at him; he wondered how many of them had spent a night or two under Margaret Corcoran's roof—and how many could identify him.

Ulysses Hill breathed evenly, pretending to be asleep when the conductor passed by again. One arm was tucked under his head, but the other was slipped under his outer coat where he could keep his hand resting lightly on the little nickel revolver. Just in case.

Once the conductor was gone, he opened his eyes and resumed staring out the window. The pale stars were obscured by high clouds, and the sliver of moon would soon slip behind the black upthrust of the Rockies. It was a winter sky.

When the conductor came through again to announce the Castle Rock stop, Hill buried his head in his hands and waited for the train to lurch to a halt. Some passengers got off, several more got on, the whistle blew, and the train edged forward, the big drivers turning faster and faster to gain purchase on the greasy rails. The pitch game picked up again.

The conductor walked through, punching the newcomers' tickets. He stopped at Hill's seat.

"The car goes to Colorado Springs, and we're right on time. Next stop, Colorado Springs, then on to Fountain and Pueblo. Scheduled arrival time in Pueblo is three-ten a.m."

Hill hunkered down a little more and smiled into the slouch hat. Even if the local police were on the alert to keep watch for him, the hour was right. It would be easy to slip away into the night and vanish.

Until the proper moment.
He stroked the nickel revolver once more.

Chapter 21

TOM ALVAREZ LAID HIS BARE HAND over the black's velvety nose and led it slowly through the undergrowth. The pale moon slipped behind a scudding cloud, and he stopped to wait for it to reappear rather than take an unnecessary chance; he'd already heard Comstock's bay snort and misstep in the darkness. When the moon slid into view again, its faint blue-white light filtering through the ponderosas, he resumed picking his way through the trees.

It was already past midnight. The long afternoon's sporadic shooting had been for naught on both sides, and after the first angry volleys, the fighting had settled into little more than the periodic crackle of gunfire that served no real purpose beyond keeping heads down on both sides.

Paine and his men held the advantage of numbers and position, but Alvarez and Comstock had made the most of their meager cover. Paine's men had been able to move easily, and they'd attempted to set up a crossfire to catch their quarry, but the two had hunkered down in the oldest part of the undergrowth. Alvarez's greatest fear had been that they'd lose their horses, but no lucky shot had claimed either animal, and after the initial excitement both the bay and the black had stood their ground placidly, perhaps because Cody's friend had picked experienced animals or perhaps because they were just worn out. Either way, Alvarez had been more than willing to accept the good luck.

Still, a smart man couldn't afford to wait out three better-armed men. The advantage of position would, in time, assure Paine his victory.

So Alvarez and Comstock were moving again, gambling on being able to sneak away under cover of night. But it was a damned risky business; a hoof snapping a dead branch, a horse whinnying, a misjudgment of direction in the darkness, or any of a dozen other mistakes would end the escape before it had properly begun.

At least they were moving. The hardest part had been the waiting, letting darkness fall and the night come on while the sharp cold of high-country winter seeped into their bones, threatening to sap the last of what energy they had left. They'd used their time to check the load in their weapons, tend their hungry horses, and eat the last of their bacon raw. Only when the moon was well past its zenith and sliding toward the high peaks of the central Rockies did they dare move out, and then only with painful, maddeningly deliberate caution.

Utter silence was the first priority, but even silence couldn't guarantee success.

Alvarez did not take a step until he was reasonably certain it was safe, and even then, he half expected to hear the zing of a bullet cutting its way through the sparse ponderosa boughs. They'd have to move away from the sheltering trees and cross whatever open ground lay ahead of them, leaving their pursuers to follow by thin starlight, but if they could find the edge of the grove before the moon set, they'd have a slim chance in the fading light to study whatever terrain they'd have to cross. And they'd have to cross a lot of country just to get to Manitou, and that would leave them fifty miles or better short of Pueblo. If they could sneak into the Springs unseen, if they could find a train with an empty boxcar headed south…

If…

Comstock's bay snorted again and Alvarez swore under his breath; he had no clear idea where Paine's left flank man was, but he could be plenty near enough to hear the bay. Alvarez patted the black horse's nose to keep it quiet. He counted to ten and moved out again.

The moon slid behind a cloud.

Somewhere high overhead, a startled owl hooted once and another answered from a long way off. Or perhaps it was the first one, already carried well beyond the ponderosas on its silent wings.

Alvarez found himself envying the owl.

Fifty yards farther on, he caught his first glimpse of the clearing when he maneuvered the black around a huge old tree. Another thirty yards, and he came to the edge of the grove. A flat grassy meadow rolled out in front of him and into a sort of narrow valley running between the foothills and the Ramparts themselves. To his right, the granite peaks loomed dark against the hazy smear of stars; to the left, the meadow fell away gently for a half mile, then sloped upward toward a little saddleback ridge. The far end was lost to sight. The line of trees curved away to the northeast and out of sight, and just where the edge of this line bent and disappeared, he saw the tiny red glow of a fire. He knew instantly that it marked the spot where at least one of Paine's men was waiting. He judged it at a third of a mile, maybe less. Plenty close enough.

The glow flared as he watched, then died down. Perhaps whoever was there had put a piece of fresh wood on the fire or had stirred the embers a little for extra warmth.

Or perhaps, Alvarez thought, he had misjudged the distance and it was only the glowing end of Paine's cigar.

No. It was fire.

He let out a breath slowly and clucked his tongue, the agreed-upon sign for Comstock, motioning him forward. There was nothing left to do now but wait for the moon to set behind the granite mountains, step out into the open and see how much distance they could put between themselves and Ted Paine before the sun came up.

Comstock and the bay nudged up alongside them.

"We walking or riding?" Comstock whispered across the bay's neck.

Alvarez scowled at him. He held up his hand and pointed two wiggling fingers downward.

Comstock gave him a sheepish grin. "Damn. Either way, I'm tore to pieces."

Alvarez shushed him and moved forward carefully until he was standing at the very edge of the shadows. He couldn't think about Comstock's wounds now. First, they had to get out of this fix. He waited for the mountains to swallow the westering moon.

"You ready, Ben?" he whispered when it was time. The words sounded as loud as gunshots in his ears.

"Ready," Comstock whispered back.

Alvarez patted the black and waited and watched the

moon disappear into the jagged mouth of the mountains. Then he stepped out of the trees and into the frosted meadow grass, heading south.

Ted Paine lowered the field glasses and rubbed his tired eyes. He'd been watching for the two old men by the last of the moonlight; once the moon was set, he knew he'd never find them.

He eased himself into the little circle of firelight and sat down cross-legged on the hard earth. "We'll break camp at sunup," he said softly. "I've got an appointment to keep elsewhere."

Dan gave Paine a funny look. "We ain't finished with our business here."

"Yes, we are. They'll be long gone by dawn."

"I can't figger you out," the little man said under his breath as he warmed his hands at the fire. A chunk of ponderosa popped hot sap, sending a shower of sparks skyward. "We could of took 'em any time we wanted this afternoon, but you wouldn't do it. 'Wait 'em out,' you said. An' now you're tellin' me they've gotten clean away."

"Or will soon. Either way, we've lost them. They're too damn cagey to stay put on a night as black as this."

"Just so you know, I don't take kindly to riskin' my neck on'y to give up for no good reason in the middle of the chase."

"You'll get paid, so I don't see you've got a beef," Paine said.

Dan eyed him across the fire. "I think you're plumb crazy," he said. "We could've took 'em." He shook his head sadly.

"Let's just say I wanted to give them a sporting

chance," Paine snapped. But in truth, he wasn't quite sure why he as letting them get away, either. Perhaps it was because he respected them. Or perhaps, like the cat who lets the mouse escape for just a moment, it was only because he wanted to prolong the thrill of the hunt.

Chapter 22

THE DAY CAME ON COLD BUT CLEAR, and the warming sun melted the frost and remnants of snow except in the gullies and shady spots. The gravediggers in Pueblo went about their work, the newspaper people gloried once more in the tall tales the pallbearers told in the saloons, and the Methodist minister went to call one more time on the Widow Toothacker to urge her to get on with the business of burying her dead.

Ulysses Hill pulled the tattered blanket around his shoulders and tried to make himself comfortable in the pile of sour old cornshucks the boardinghouse mistress had given him for a mattress. The thin-lipped old woman had turned him down for a room because he had no money, but her ugly daughter had taken pity on him because of his deformity and offered him shelter in their barn.

Every part of him ached for sleep, but he knew he didn't dare nod off: Pueblo was crawling with policemen, and if the woman got wind that they were looking for him, she'd call the law in a flash.

He patted the little revolver in his pocket.

A rat crept out of the straw on the far side of the barn and stood up on its hindquarters, its black nose twitching as it sampled the air to take in all the new scents associated with this interloper in its domain.

Hill pulled the revolver out of his pocket slows and stretched it out in front of him.

"Bang" he said.

The rat whirled and scurried back to the safety of its nest in the straw. He smiled and pulled the gun up to his face, feeling the cool metal on his cheek. Then he put his head down in the straw and drifted into sleep with the gun still cradled in his hand.

Bill Tilghman looked up from his newspaper to see the tall, white-maned showman stroll through the lobby, a little knot of grimy children moving alongside, hanging on his every word just as their steelworker fathers had the night before. It struck Tilghman suddenly that these kids would grow up associating Buffalo Bill with the West's early years, and he was surprised that it didn't rankle him. Maybe it was just as well that they'd remember the beautiful lies rather than the gritty, common-man truth.

Cody dug into his pockets and handed each of the boys a penny, then he shooed them out the door and told them to get on to school.

Wyatt Earp snorted and sprawled in the chair next to Tilghman's. "I don't care if I never see that old buzzard again!"

"I suspect it'll all be over tomorrow," Tilghman said carefully. He returned to his paper.

Earp wouldn't be ignored. He put out a bony finger and pushed the newspaper aside. "Where the hell's Masterson? I want to play me some cards."

"You know where he is," the Oklahoman said quietly.

"You ask me, Alvarez and Comstock are deader'n door nails. We're waitin' on a couple of dead men." He grinned, showing long white teeth in the wide mouth. "If you ask me."

Tilghman trained his pale gray eyes on Earp's sharp features. "No one asked you, Wyatt."

Gertrude Toothacker knew these latest visitors were coming long before she heard the shuffling of their horses in her yard or their boots scraping on her stoop. Tilghman, Masterson, and the others had warned her to be on the lookout for them, but of course that wasn't necessary at all; she was attuned to such quiet comings and goings, had developed a sixth sense about them from a lifetime of putting up with Arnold's periodic absences and sudden returns.

She pulled herself out of her overstuffed green chair, wrapped her gray shawl around her shoulders against the chill, and went to wait for them in the darkened kitchen where she would watch them coming up the pathway from the alley behind her outbuildings, leading two of the most worn-out, sorry-looking horses she'd ever seen. Even in the warm yellow light of afternoon, the men looked gray and haggard as they limped along, but now that they were here, she could get on with the burial.

The recognition that all this would soon be over caught her almost by surprise, as it had many times over the past few days. She had done those countless little things that were expected of a new widow—endless chores, attending to the thousand funeral details, entertaining this bunch of his former comrades or that bunch of old biddies from her church circle—without stopping to think much about what lay ahead. Now that reality was upon her.

Most of all, she missed Arnold. She wondered how long it would be before she could go to bed at night and, in the moments before sleep, not reach out for him or be surprised that he wasn't there. How long would she pour two morning cups of coffee before remembering he wouldn't be padding in from the bedroom all hung over and apologetic?

Well, the snow had melted and the grave was dug. Tomorrow this part, at least, would be over.

Perhaps then she'd have some rest.

But first she would have to look after these newcomers.

She got down cups and saucers, poured the coffee, and waited for them.

Two old reprobates. Lawmen become outlaws over the nasty business surrounding her husband's death. Still, in all her years with Arnold, she'd never heard him utter a word against these two. Arnold had had tremendous respect for both of them, and while he had many faults, being a poor judge of character wasn't one of them. She knew deep in her soul that if they were half the men she thought they were, neither Ben Comstock nor Tom Alvarez would break the spirit of the law, even if their responsibilities forced them to tamper with the letter of it now and again. To rare and tough old birds such as these, the law was a god, and upholding its tenets their whole reason for existence.

Which, when she reflected on it, was why she'd been proud to put up with Arnold all these years.

And now they were coming to help avenge his death.

They came into her yard and tethered their animals at the rain barrel twenty yards from the house. The bare-headed one needed help stepping onto her porch, and she felt a little twinge of shock at seeing Ben Comstock look so haggard.

Still, she let them rap twice before she opened the door.

"Hello, Mrs. Toothacker. Our condolences on your loss." Ben Comstock leaned against the doorframe and licked his cracked lips, his face almost colorless beneath the grime. "Don't know if you remember us. We're old friends of your husband's. We come to see him off."

"I remember you," she said. Up close, she could see he was trembling with fever.

Tom Alvarez took off his big black hat and turned it over in his hands. "Gertrude, it's good to see you again." She remembered he always had been a man of few words and fewer emotions. Not a bad combination, all in all.

Comstock blinked. "You haven't had the services yet, have you?"

"Not yet. Tomorrow," she said.

"Then we're in time."

"You are."

Alvarez cleared his throat. "Gertrude, there are some matters you ought to be aware of…" He made eye contact for a split second and then turned to look over his shoulder down the long path they'd followed to her door.

"You mean the trouble you're in? I know all about that. Bill Tilghman told me."

Alvarez nodded. "Is he here?"

"He'll be by later. Take your boots off here by the door."

Comstock stumbled across the threshold and nearly fell.

"He's damn sick," Alvarez said.

She saw the dried blood on his trousers. "I can see that." She nodded toward Comstock. "After I get him fed, I'll fetch Bill Tilghman. He'll want to know you're here. I'll get a doctor, too."

"No doctor," Comstock protested weakly. His eyes came open, showing whites the color of egg yolk. "Don't want no damn doctor. Can't trust 'em." He thrust his chin out in defiance, lost his balance, and caught himself on a kitchen chair.

"You'll have to," she said.

Ted Paine paced the paneled room angrily. He smelled of woodsmoke and pine needles, and a little cloud of dust rose from his heavy coat with each step. A young man in a starched white shirt and ill-fitting black suit watched him.

"Mr. Dahlman says he'll be back in a minute," the young man sniffed.

"I know, dammit!" Paine snapped. He stopped at the cherrywood desk and picked up a fancy silver inkwell and read the inscription: Horace Dahlman, Esq.

"Leave it alone," Dahlman said from the doorway.

Paine whirled and saw the big man. "About time," he said.

Dahlman gave him a thin smile. "That will be all, Roger," he said to the young man without looking at him.

"Is there anything else I can get for you, sir?" The young man seemed reluctant to leave.

"Not at all, Roger. You may go." The big man eased himself into the leather office chair and pulled a penknife out of the desk drawer and began cleaning his fingernails.

"Thank you, Mr. Dahlman." Roger gave Paine another suspicious glance and slipped out of the room.

The big man waited until the door closed. "Now, Theodore. What happened?"

Paine held his temper in check. "I don't know how the bastards got away," he said. "Shouldn't have happened, but it did." He stopped at the ornate cherrywood desk and took a cigar out of the humidor, bit off the end, and struck a match on his trousers. Once the cigar was going, he let the match fall to the floor and ground it into the parquet with his heel. "We had them in a good crossfire half the day, and my trackers are the best in the business. As soon as we discovered they were gone, we hightailed it for the Springs and caught the train. A brakeman said he'd seen two old codgers on fagged-out horses around the yards at midmorning, so I assume they got here ahead of us."

Dahlman flicked a fingernail paring off his black trousers. "It seems to me your trackers couldn't find their buttocks with both hands. But then perhaps you don't agree," he said quietly. He closed the knife and slid it into the drawer.

"We just lost them," Paine said.

The big man's eyes closed all the way as he brought both hands up to his face and tapped his fingertips together lightly. "That may be, Theodore, that may be. Nevertheless, I can't help thinking you've made a great many mistakes in this matter." The eyes opened, found Paine, and held him. "I heard you let them get away."

"Bullshit," Paine snapped.

A sort of smile played across Dahlman's small mouth, but there was no humor at all in his voice as he said, "Mistakes have been made, and you'll be held accountable. I can't afford another."

Paine leaned across the desk at him and blew smoke in his face. "Just remember this was your idea from the first, you fat bastard. You were the one who came to me, wanting that girl killed, remember? The great Horace Dahlman couldn't run for governor unless he got that certain *embarrassment* out of the way!"

"But you took my money to do the deed. Is that not so? Then you hired that cripple and assured me there would be no mistakes. Is that not also true? All he had to do was kill her and dispose of the one trinket that could link her to me. Instead, he stole it for himself. You could have prevented it, Theodore, but you did not. To top it off, you had that drunkard killed." Dahlman pushed himself away from the desk and stood. "That was absolutely unnecessary. You should have found the brooch, disposed of it, and put Toothacker on trial. He would have been acquitted on the basis of his past reputation, and that would have been that. But you made a mistake." He reached out and took the cigar from Paine's mouth. "Now, the cripple is on the run and those two bulldog lawmen have the brooch."

Pained turned away under the pressure of the big man's gaze. "We'll still get them," he muttered.

"We'd better, Theodore. We'd better. That is, you will if you know what's good for you."

"Yes, sir," Paine said through clenched teeth.

Dahlman settled back into his chair and closed his eyes. "I'll see you at the funeral, then." A wide, soft grin, utterly genuine now, spread across Dahlman's florid face, giving him the look of a cat that had just finished dining on a most succulent mouse. He moved his right hand slowly to his ample stomach and tucked his fingers into his vest watch pocket. "After all, any candidate for governor worth his salt should be prominent among the mourners for one of Colorado's most famous lawmen, don't you think?"

Bat Masterson and Wyatt Earp waited down the lane from the Toothacker house and kept watch from the rented buggy while Bill Tilghman and the doctor trudged up the hill to pay their respects to the widow. Night was falling, and the temperature was dropping with the fading light. Autumn was gone in the high country and fading rapidly from the plains.

Masterson glanced around the buggy top to see what had become of the local constable who'd drawn up a quarter of a mile down the road. The young policeman sat there, too far away to see what was going on, yet too close to avoid detection. He'd seemed like a nice kid when they'd made his acquaintance at the hotel. Earnest and hardworking. In the long run, he'd be a hopeless failure as a lawman.

For his own part, Masterson wished this business were finished so he could get back to New York and the easy life. He'd give up this cold Colorado weather and the company of cranky old-timers in a minute just to be back in the geometric perfection of the baseball diamond or the smoky, genteel dankness of ringside at the prizefights.

Earp pulled his coat collar up around his scrawny neck to ward off the night chill. "Wish those sonsabitches'd hurry," he said. "We've wasted enough time on this caper."

Masterson sniffed. "Unless I miss my guess, this caper'll be done with soon enough. We'll be laying Arnold Toothacker to rest tomorrow morning, and whatever's going to happen will happen then."

"That's what Tilghman said."

"He's right."

Earp turned toward him and grinned, his teeth showing in the darkness. "You think there'll be gunplay?" He smelled of liver and onions and fine cologne. Once, he'd been a dandy, the smartest and most dangerous man in the West. Now he seemed a caricature of himself.

But Masterson wasn't about to cross him. With Wyatt, it always came down to this. Do or die, and hang the consequences. "I suppose. It seems that's what it's all building up to."

Earp cleared his throat and spat into the road. "Be a damn waste of time sittin' around here if we don't get a chance to let off a little steam, wouldn't it?"

Chapter 23

Tom Alvarez stood at the kitchen window with a cup of Gertrude Toothacker's good strong coffee cradled in his hands and watched the first lavender smear of sunrise give form and depth to the eastern horizon. He had slept well, thanks to a wonderful meal of pork roast and turnips—and the solid assurances of assistance from steady old Bill Tilghman.

He always marveled at his own recuperative powers. Maybe he wasn't so old after all. Now he felt better than he had in weeks.

Except for the deep, warning ache in his bad leg.

This morning, though, he scarcely noticed. Dangerous things needed doing, and if the leg served to remind him of his own frailty, so much the better. No matter how rested and ready he felt, it was only prudent to remember his limitations.

Ben Comstock shuffled into the kitchen in his stockinged feet. His eyes were still red with fever and the crepelike skin around them was jaundice yellow, but he seemed stronger. Sleep had helped him, as had the doctor's ministrations and the foul-smelling poultice he'd prescribed.

"How do you feel?" Alvarez asked.

Comstock grunted and settled gingerly into a kitchen chair. "It'll take more than a little buckshot and a hard ride to put someone as tough as me out of commission. Where's the widow?"

Alvarez cocked his head toward the parlor, where she sat rocking silently in the darkness. Only her marble-white hands, folded tightly in her lap, were visible against the black of her dress.

"She's been there since I got up," Alvarez said, feeling vaguely uneasy talking about the woman when she was close enough to hear him. "I reckon she's making peace with her loss."

Comstock scratched himself. "S'pose it's a good thing to do. Makes it easier in the end. Or so I'm told." He kept his voice soft and low, out of respect for the grieving.

Alvarez poured Comstock a cup of coffee from the pot simmering on the woodstove. "I thought I'd fix us some bacon and flapjacks. She says she doesn't want any but doesn't mind if we have some."

"Tough woman," Comstock offered. "Hotcakes would be damn good, to tell you the truth. If she don't mind." He blew across the coffee to cool it. "What time we leaving for the funeral?"

"Eleven," Alvarez answered, digging through her cupboards for the breakfast makings. The baking powder and flour were in bins, the butter and eggs in an oaken pie safe. He could cook a camp meal as well as any man and better than most, but in a woman's kitchen he was lost.

He lined the ingredients up and rooted around some more for a big bowl. "There's no church service. Just the graveside. But you're staying put. Doctor's orders."

"The hell I am," Comstock said. "I didn't come all this way to miss my chance at them bastards, damn it! I'm going to be there."

Alvarez cracked eggs, getting more shell into the bowl than he could pick out with his thick fingers. "You ain't going."

"You ain't man enough to stop me, Thomas. Not now, not ever." There was no malice in the way he said it, just determination. He slurped down the rest of his coffee.

"You need to rest. The exertion could kill you."

Comstock set the cup down almost daintily. "You should understand this better'n anyone. The shame of letting some bastard get away with murder when I can do something about it might just kill me, too. I ain't never been shamed by anyone, and I won't start now."

"Paine'll be there. You know that. He's expecting us."

"Good. I'd hate to have it any other way." Comstock leaned back against the wall. "Don't misunderstand me, Thomas. I don't hanker to die. No sane man does. But I'd rather go all at once than sit here turning to rot. Especially if I've got a chance to even up a couple of past-due accounts, if you get my drift."

Alvarez shifted his weight to his good leg. He got the drift, all right. This was what they'd come for, after all. There wasn't a power on earth that could keep him from the cemetery. He'd never believed in revenge as a motive, probably because he'd never had occasion to be vengeful; it was an emotion that could cloud a man's judgment just when he needed it most, placing him in needless danger.

But he had to admit that this time he wanted revenge. Ted Paine had made this personal. Every part of his body was tense with anticipation. And fear. Like the ache in his leg, that was a good sign. A little fear sharpened the senses.

He glanced over his shoulder at Comstock. Ben was truly an old man now, but even as sick as he was, he needed this showdown, this settling of old scores for Arnold and new scores for himself, deep down in his soul.

Alvarez cracked another egg, this time perfectly.

Maybe it would be a very good day after all.

Autumn-browned grass crunched underfoot, and the last dirty remnants of snow in the shadows of the pines ringing the cemetery melted away to nothingness in the warm, dry air. The black horse-drawn hearse rolled up the rough gravel road and through the open wrought-iron gate into the hillside cemetery. Mourners followed on foot, the boots of the men and the dainty black high-button shoes of the women gone dirty brown from the mud in the road, the black worsted trousers and mourning dresses spattered by horses' hooves and iron-tired hearse wheels. The Methodist minister, short and fat with the dour look of a man whose breakfast had disagreed with him, led the little procession. His great girth pressed against his vest, preventing his swallowtail coat from closing, and the tails flapped in the warm morning breeze as he walked. He reminded Tom Alvarez of a stout magpie strutting along in front of a flock of lesser blackbirds.

The widow, walking alone, came along a few paces behind, and the pallbearers, including Theodore Paine, and the other mourners followed her. An honor guard of blue-suited riflemen, undoubtedly there for the final salute of arms, paused at the wrought-iron entry gate and let the cortege proceed to the gravesite.

Alvarez leaned back against a pink granite obelisk and waited. This was tricky business. The old pioneer graveyard was out in an open area carved out of a stand of timber, and the freeze-and-thaw cycle of hard foothill winters had tipped many of the larger marble monuments at crazy angles. It would take some careful doing to slip unnoticed into the little knot of mourners, and he was glad he and Comstock had decided against accompanying Gertrude Toothacker to the undertaker's. There was freedom of movement here, and there wasn't any doubt they'd need it.

He only hoped there wouldn't be too much commotion. But then, perhaps old Arnold, at least, would understand.

He pulled his Smith and Wesson out of his coat pocket and inspected it carefully. A sheen of fresh oil coated the blued barrel. The clumsy old gun had never failed him in all the years he'd carried it, precisely because he took such great care to assure himself that it was in working order. He opened the cylinder and loaded a sixth shell into the one empty chamber, then snapped it shut and laid his thumb on the hammer. He'd loved the smell of oil and black powder and lead all his life.

He was ready.

The hearse creaked to a stop and waited for the mourners to catch up. The minister tugged at the swallowtails, mopped his brow, and said something to the driver as he passed. The driver snapped the reins and the horses moved forward. They were within a hundred yards of Arnold Toothacker's final resting place now, and it was only seemly that the man of God should arrive first to welcome the empty husk of the dearly departed to the eternal grave.

Instinctively, Alvarez crouched a little, taking care to keep himself behind the granite. The stone was cold to the touch; as he waited, he traced the legend carved delicately into the stone with the fingertips of his left hand:

> Dearest Mother
> Rest in Peace
> June 6, 1870-March 18, 1903

Too young to die, Alvarez thought. But then so many of them were. Motherhood was a dangerous gamble in the best of times and the best of places. His fingers traced on.

> Infant Daughter
> Beloved, Not Lost
> March 18, 1903

Such human frailty always made him wonder how it had come to be that he'd been singled out for such a long life in spite of the daily dangers he'd faced while others' lives were snuffed out even before they'd begun. The thought made the hairs on the back of his neck stand up. It was the luck of the draw, that's all. When your string's up, it's up.

He pulled his hand from the cold stone and turned to watch the funeral procession as it labored up the slight grade. The mourners were just coming even with Comstock's hiding place behind a fancy granite mausoleum erected by one of Pueblo's prominent pioneer families. Almost unconsciously, Alvarez reached into his trouser pocket and felt the smoothness and filigree of the bluestone brooch.

Ulysses Hill trudged the final mile without being seen by another living soul as far as he could tell, which was exactly as he wanted it. There was too much to do, too much at stake to get caught now.

Once he crossed the tracks and passed through the mill yards and began moving up the long hill toward the cemetery, he relaxed a little and widened his stride. A lone man afoot stirred little interest among grazing cattle and a few fenced-in horses.

He'd spent the better part of the previous night wrapped in his thin coat, waiting in the shadows outside the funeral parlor, hoping to spot his prey, but the wait had been fruitless, and he'd had to console himself with the notion that the cemetery would be far better for what he had in mind, anyway. The granite and marble in the graveyard would at least give him cover and permit him to get close enough for a killing shot with his little pocket pistol.

He smiled as he walked.

More than anything else, there was a certain justice in knowing the end would come here, among the dead.

One way or the other.

He followed the last curve of the muddy road, saw the cadre of police lounging at the gate before they saw him, and angled into the trees. Working his way farther uphill through the windbreak pines, he cut back into the cemetery when he figured it was safe. He could see the funeral party, their backs turned to him. His heart was pounding hard and he took a deep breath to clear his lungs and head.

Leather creaked and wood slid on wood: the pallbearers were removing the casket from the wagon box.

He pulled out the little pocket pistol, crept around a stone marker, ran in a half-squat to another, and then to a third. This last marker was weathered marble, barely four feet high and within a dozen yards of a wedge of scraggly timber that marked the cemetery boundary. He knelt and peered around the stone, being careful to reveal as little of himself as possible.

Only then did he see another crouched form stand up and slip into the cluster of mourners.

It was Tom Alvarez.

The minister planted himself at the head of the casket and thumbed through a worn Bible while the mourners found their places around the rectangular gash in the earth.

Someone cleared his throat impatiently and a woman blew her nose.

Everything was ready.

The minister nodded solemnly, and Colonel William Frederick Cody took off his high-crowned hat out of respect for the dead and stepped forward, pulling a little sheaf of papers from a coat pocket as he moved past the preacher. Out of the corner of his eye, Cody saw Alvarez moving along the rear of the gathering, but he showed neither recognition nor surprise; a rapturous smile played across his handsome features, and he turned and offered a little bow of condolence to the widow.

He took a deep breath and began his farewell to Arnold Toothacker.

Police Commissioner Theodore Paine felt the presence of danger like a cold breath on the back of his neck even before the pallbearers had heaved the casket onto the low sawhorses and threaded the lowering ropes through the pulleys. He took a quick glance to his left: Horace Dahlman and his lady stood quietly with bowed heads, apparently absorbed in the first booming words from Cody's lips. His glance jumped to the other pallbearers. No problem there. Five old men, once tough as saddle leather, now gone soft and slow.

Then, out of the corner of his eye, he saw a flutter of quick movement to his right, a hesitation, and then movement again. He knew instantly who it was.

So the waiting was over.

Cody's baritone flowed across the hilltop. "Our friend Arnold, so rudely snatched from our midst…"

Paine drew back his mourning coat and touched the wooden handle of the Colt Peacemaker at his waist.

"… will stand before Thy divine throne this hour, his soul in Thy care, awaiting Thy judgment…"

Now, Paine thought. *Now.*

He took three quick side steps toward a fat pink-granite carving of a sleeping lamb and started to turn to his right, his hand ready to snatch his weapon from its scabbard. But something to his left moved, where he hadn't expected it.

He swung around.

It was Comstock, coming his way, his eyes brooding and menacing.

Paine's mind raced. Caught between them! He pushed off the marble monument, ready to run, but a split second too late.

Tom Alvarez was on him, jamming the hard nose of his revolver into his ribs.

Alvarez leaned into him. "Don't move unless I tell you to."

"Nice to see you, Commissioner," Comstock hissed, and he wrapped his big hands around Paine's upper arm as he sidled up alongside him. The grip was like iron bands cutting into his flesh.

Bill Cody's voice rose and fell with the prayer's refrain. "The peace of God, which passeth all understanding..."

Paine looked Alvarez straight into the eye. "You two are dead men," he whispered.

"Amen!" Cody pronounced, and the mourners raised their heads. Bill Tilghman saw them, and a self-satisfied little smile touched the corners of his mouth, turning up the ends of his mustache. He nudged Bat Masterson as the minister stepped forward solemnly and Buffalo Bill moved aside.

"Thank you, Colonel," the minister intoned, his thin voice sounding even weaker after Cody's easy delivery. "Now, my brothers and sisters, let us commend our brother Arnold to the dust from which he came." He opened his Bible and began to read the chosen text.

Comstock tightened his grip. "We'll take you to hell with us," he said, too loudly.

The minister paused at the interruption he couldn't quite identify and cleared his throat. The widow looked up, found Alvarez and Comstock, and flushed with anger.

"Beg pardon, ma'am," Alvarez said, and he touched the brim of his hat by way of apology. He pulled his coat over the Smith and Wesson and moved to one side, placing himself deliberately between Ted Paine and the mourners, with his back to the coffin.

He waited for the minister to pick up where he'd left off before he spoke again. "Who killed the girl?" he asked so softly even Comstock barely heard him.

Paine heard, though; his eyes snapped with fury.

Alvarez whispered, "You killed the girl and Arnold. Or had them killed. We want to know why."

Paine only hawked phlegm and spat it onto Alvarez's boots.

Comstock gave the arm a sharp twist that sent a stabbing pain through his victim's shoulder, and leaned close to Paine's ear. "Tell him or I'll break it off, you bastard!"

The minister stopped in midsentence. "Gentlemen, in the name of all that's holy…"

Comstock twisted again, and Paine's knees buckled as he tried to jerk his arm free. Across the way, he saw Horace Dahlman watching intently. "Tell him!" Comstock twisted again.

"Why don't you ask *him*," Paine said, and he looked straight at Dahlman. "Ask the fat bastard over there!"

Alvarez spun around in time to see Dahlman, his face deathly white, look away.

"Him?" Comstock barked. "He's the one?"

A rumble like summer thunder moved through the crowd, leaving the minister sputtering in its wake. The widow was on her feet, coming toward them, but Bill Cody reached out a hand and took her by the shoulder and guided her gently to her seat.

"Him!" Paine shouted, but Comstock only twisted harder. Dahlman's thin wife gave the three of them a quizzical little smile and reached for her husband. The mourners were all moving now in spite of the minister's entreaties for order.

Alvarez's heart seemed to skip a beat with the sudden realization that he had what he'd come for. He slipped the bluestone brooch from his pocket and stepped forward and laid it delicately on the polished coffin wood for all to see. "Begging your forgiveness, ma'am," he said to Gertrude, "but this was something the departed would have wanted me to do." The silver caught and reflected the late morning sun.

Dahlman's wife sucked in her breath, and her hands went to her throat. She started to say something to her husband, but he brushed her off and took a step in Paine's direction. Bill Tilghman, seeing the threat, swung out of line toward him.

"For the love of God, please!" the minister begged. "Let us have order!" But the assemblage paid him no attention as they crowded together, away from the three angry-looking men who had started the commotion. Someone bumped into the coffin, sending it sliding off the pulleys and nosing into the ground at an odd angle. The bluestone brooch rattled down the side of the box and disappeared into the soft earth.

Someone else swore and a woman shrieked. From down the hill came the cadre of blue-uniformed policemen, moving on the double.

Only Theodore Paine saw the hunched form step out of the trees.

In one smooth motion, Paine shoved Ben Comstock hard, sending him sprawling. Then he dropped to his knees, drew his Colt from its holster, and swung it up a split second before he saw the puff of smoke that came simultaneously with the sharp pop of the gun. He squeezed the Colt's trigger without aiming. It bucked in his hand, and the boom ricocheted off a hundred carved headstones.

Comstock started to get up, but Paine swung the barrel

of the Colt across Comstock's eyes and he fell back, stunned.

Paine cocked the hammer, turned, and squeezed the trigger again, sending a slug toward Alvarez. The bullet struck a cockeyed marker: a pink granite Easter lily crowning the stone exploded, showering Alvarez in a cloud of dust. He ducked behind the stone and wiped the back of his hand across his cheeks. It came away bloody.

A shrill police whistle filled the air before the gunshot died away.

The place was pandemonium. Tilghman and Cody pulled Gertrude Toothacker away and snapped out orders for the other pallbearers to move the mourners toward cover. The minister flailed his arms and screamed for the police. Earp and Masterson, crouching low, dodged among the headstones toward Paine, but he snapped off a round, pinning them down, and headed for Dahlman. The big man turned and started to run just as the little gun at the edge of the woods popped again. A bullet meant for Ted Paine crashed into Dahlman's shoulder. He fell to his knees as his wife tried in vain to hold him up.

And then Paine was upon them.

Tom Alvarez stared at the Smith and Wesson in his hands and raised the cool barrel to his lips, touching the blade sight to his forehead.

He thumbed back the hammer and fired, as the blood pounded hot in his temples.

Chapter 24

PAINE DODGED ALVAREZ'S FIRST SHOT as he vaulted the open grave and bore down on Horace Dahlman. In two strides he'd kicked the big man out of the way and caught his horrified wife and spun her around to use as a shield.

The Pueblo police, lumbering uphill in close order, had their weapons out and trained on Alvarez as they came on, but another pop of the .32 in the trees knocked a constable to his knees. The sergeant blew his whistle again and the troop charged off after the retreating Ulysses Hill.

"Let the woman go!" Alvarez shouted. He was going for Paine, crouching as low as his bad leg would permit, and Paine squeezed off a round in his direction, missing. Mrs. Dahlman struggled, but Paine put the muzzle of his Colt to her temple.

Dahlman growled something and snatched at Paine's leg, earning him another kick in the ribs. A crimson stain was spreading slowly outward from Dahlman's left shoulder across the front of his white shirt, and his face was the dead white of dirty snow.

"Let her go, dammit!" Alvarez had the Smith and Wesson aimed point blank at Paine, but he didn't dare squeeze the trigger, and they both knew it.

Paine grinned and started to take his own aim, but off to his left he saw two pallbearers break away from the mourners and angle in his direction.

One was short and round, the other tall and arrow thin. Masterson and Earp.

Two more who could shoot straight.

He kept his Colt at full cock and backpedaled toward the woods, dragging the woman with him.

Ben Comstock knelt on the turf and eyed the trees as Paine and the woman disappeared with Earp and Masterson and Alvarez close on their heels. Behind him, he heard the frightened murmur of the crowd as Cody and John Poe moved everyone away, and above it all, Gertrude Toothacker's voice, strong and clear, refusing to move. He turned and saw Bill Tilghman pulling her away gently. She raged at him for a moment, but then her natural dignity seemed to return and she gave up and let him lead her to a safer spot.

Damn fine woman, that one. He felt a twinge of regret that they'd ruined her final moments with Arnold. But he knew Arnold would have wanted it this way.

In spite of the buzzing in his head, the fatigue of fever that had hung on him like a millstone was gone. He inhaled the smell of burnt powder and pushed himself to his feet. His nose was bleeding, but he wiped at it once and promptly forgot about it.

There were things that needed doing.

He scrambled for the woods, got halfway there, and turned back toward the open grave and the fat man lying beside it.

Comstock towered over him. "I'll be damned if I'll leave garbage like you behind!" He grabbed him by the collar and pulled so hard against the three-hundred-pound weight the fine fabric tore in his hand.

Dahlman gave him a sour look. "You're crazy," he said, but it was mock defiance.

Comstock got a better grip and found the strength to yank Dahlman upright, holding him out like a prize hunting trophy. "I've still got a score to settle with Theodore Paine, bur you're comin' along to watch!"

"I'm shot," the man protested. Fresh blood leaked out of his shoulder wound, and his knees started to give out again.

"You're shot in the shoulder, you sonofabitch. There ain't a damn thing wrong with your legs! Besides, this way you can see what your friend's done with your wife, if you care." He shoved the man hard, caught him when he stumbled, and kept him moving into the sheltering of the trees.

The woods ran along the crest of the hill and down the other side for some distance before petering out in broad flats west of the rail yard. Beyond the tracks lay the roaring coke furnaces and belching smokestacks of the steel mill set like an ugly cancer against the foothills.

Golden round aspen leaves rained down on them as they pushed through the stands of thin, straight trees and skirted the scrub oak thickets. While Comstock dragged Dahlman along, Alvarez took the point, studying the ground as they went, with Earp moving easily on the left flank and the fat Masterson wheezing along on the right. The tracking was easy thanks to the soft earth.

After a quarter of a mile, Alvarez found the woman's tracks, veering off alone, heading south for twenty yards, then circling in apparent confusion before doubling back toward the cemetery; Paine had let her go. Alvarez called a halt.

"Bat, you peel off and find her," he said.

Masterson wiped a forearm across his sweaty face. He looked relieved as he turned and shuffled off, following the woman's meandering track. "See you boys later, then," he called over his shoulder.

"He'll only slow us up, anyway," Earp observed.

Alvarez gave him a sharp look. "This ain't your fight, either," he said. "We can take it from here."

"And miss all the fun? Not on your life. Now come on, time's wasting."

"The point is, nobody invited you, Wyatt," Comstock said.

"The point is, you might just need my help whether you want it or not," Earp shot back.

Alvarez shrugged and started searching the wide track again, leaving the two of them to argue while they followed along deeper into the woods.

Ahead of them, the police had split up and regrouped several times in pursuit of Ulysses Hill. In some places, the pungent smell of burnt powder still hung in the air, and in one little clearing, Alvarez and the others found six small-caliber brass shell casings still warm to the touch.

Alvarez got down on his hands and knees to study the sign.

Comstock was puffing now from the exertion of pulling Dahlman along, and he seemed glad for a breather. "What do you see, Thomas?"

Dahlman's legs started to give out.

"Keep your feet, you damn bag of blubber!" Comstock warned, and he gave his prisoner's arm a sharp twist.

The air went out of Dahlman, and he whined something about being hurt, but he kept his feet.

Comstock twisted the arm again for emphasis. "Dammit, what are you lookin' for, Thomas?"

"Sign," Alvarez said.

Earp was looking over his shoulder. "Don't wait too damn long. I'd bet there's more law coming."

Alvarez straightened up. Wyatt was probably right. He hurried on, fanning out from the main track and working both sides in an arc. On a bare patch of ground he found the scuff marks of feet, and a few yards farther on, he saw a single small boot print in the mud.

"Look at this," he said, pointing out the way the print deepened toward the outside of the foot rather than at the ball and heel.

Earp peered at it while Comstock caught up. "What's it mean?"

Alvarez found another print to be sure. Whoever had made the track was walking or running with an odd gait. "Ulysses Hill," he said. "He split off here. Or hid and they missed him." He searched the ground for another print, found one, and then another. "The rest of them went around that big oak and kept going that way—"

"Northeast," Earp said.

Alvarez nodded. "Northeast. But Hill went straight east from here."

"What about Paine?" Comstock asked.

Alvarez scratched his head. "I don't know. Maybe he sneaked in with the others once he got shed of the woman.

Or maybe we missed him somewhere along the way."

"You mean he could be behind us?"

Alvarez nodded.

"Shit," Comstock said. "Which way now?"

The report of a big police revolver rolled up the hillside to them, followed a second later by the little pop of a small weapon.

"Sounds like it's a running fight to me," Earp said.

Alvarez considered it for only a moment. It struck him suddenly that his bad leg didn't hurt at all. He helped Comstock prod Dahlman into moving, and together they headed downhill toward the sound of the gunfire.

Paine clambered to the top of a rust-red ore pile and flopped face-down into the dust and broken-rock talus just as another small-caliber round thudded into the dirt ten feet in front of him. The black smoke from a police fusillade hung in the air around him. When he looked up, he saw Ulysses Hill taking shelter forty yards away.

Too many of the police were wasting their time scouring the railroad tracks and checking every ore car and coal hopper within sight when the enemy was right here, within their grasp, but what was done couldn't be undone at the moment.

"Still and all, I've got you now, Ulysses Hill," he said out loud. "The high ground wins!"

He smiled and brought his big Colt around to sight in on his target. Just one good shot and he'd bag his one last chance of salvaging this thing. Just one good shot at the scapegoat...

That was when he saw the other men loping through the slag and coke piles. Four big men.

A policeman saw them, too, and shouted something. They stopped, then split up, with two dragging Horace Dahlman along toward Hill's position while Wyatt Earp headed toward the ore pile, his hands over his head, keeping himself between the police and the other three.

But Earp, the bastard, didn't count on Paine having the vantage point of the high ground!

Paine aimed the Colt at Tom Alvarez and squeezed the trigger, just a fraction of a second too late. Unharmed, the three disappeared behind a rusting pile of scrap iron. "Damn!" he said, and he eyed Earp. The police had him surrounded, but he was talking easily, waving his hands, and there was no damn doubt that they recognized him. He'd be free as a jaybird in a minute, and Paine knew the Pueblo police would side with Earp over him. He slid away from the ore pile. This was going to take some thought.

Ulysses Hill trained his small gun on Alvarez, Comstock, and their captive, Dahlman. They were puffing and wheezing from the run.

"What the hell are you doing here?" he asked, waving the nickel-plated revolver around.

"What the hell do you think?" Comstock said coldly.

Hill cocked his piece. "You aren't going to arrest me. I'll kill you first."

Alvarez couldn't help a dry laugh. "Looks to me like we're all running a hell of a risk of dying. Ted Paine wants us as bad as those Pueblo boys want you right now. We just want some answers."

Hill stabbed the gun in Dahlman's direction. "Why's he here?"

"Same reason," Comstock snapped. "So we can get

some answers before those guns out there cut us down."

"You got it all figured out already, don't you?"

"Not all of it," Alvarez said. "You already told us you killed the girl and that Paine hired you. We want to know why."

The hunchback met his gaze but couldn't hold it.

Comstock prodded Dahlman. "Paine says it was this fat bastard. He wasn't lyin', was he?"

Hill stared hard at the fat man and slowly shook his head. "I don't know."

"Sure you do," Alvarez said. "Now tell us why your friend here wanted the girl killed. Whores are a minor embarrassment at best. What could have made an important man bother with bribing a police commissioner to kill a whore? What did Paine tell you?"

"Take care of the girl for an important man. That's all he said."

"That's all?"

"That's all." But of course it wasn't all. Hill looked from one man to another, and after a moment his chest seemed to swell with something like pride. His eyes stopped on Dahlman's. "But I knew who was paying. And I knew why. The 'important man' was planning to run for governor in nineteen-twelve. Everyone knew it. He had his machine in place, and the votes were all but counted. Only one possible embarrassment stood in his way. The Morgan girl. She was an opium-eater, and he was the one who'd gotten it for her. She told me that herself. I think she was proud just knowing a man as important as him. She lorded it over all of us and told everyone she was his mistress." He paused, then looked at Alvarez. "That's why he wanted her dead. Besides, she had something of value that belonged to him."

"The brooch."

Dahlman coughed and tried to squirm away, but Comstock planted his shoe against his bloodied shoulder and pushed him over into the cinders.

Hill nodded. "I was supposed to steal the trinket, too. Since Toothacker was passed out in the room when I killed her, I decided to make it look like he did it."

Comstock aimed the .38 at the bridge of Dahlman's nose. "What about killing Arnold? And setting us up?"

Dahlman licked his lips. "That was Paine's doing, not mine. After Toothacker started talking about the brooch Paine decided—" Before he could complete the sentence, a volley of shots ripped through the tangled scrap, ricocheting in a half dozen directions. Alvarez and Comstock ducked, but Ulysses Hill spun and emptied his weapon in the direction of the firing.

"Don't waste your damn lead," Comstock barked.

Hill only gave him an ugly look, then reloaded and fired again, this time into the air, until the weapon dry-snapped.

The shots were answered with more whistling lead.

Paine crouched low as he ran the wide semicircle through the piles of coke and furnace refuse, around the big alloy ladles smelling of burnt raw metal. He ducked behind a slowly turning auger carrying coke to the furnace, and somewhere off to his left the mill belched out a wave of noise and heat. His heart was racing wildly. The police fired another salvo, and the hunchback and the two old men responded.

So far so good. But he couldn't count on the support

much longer. Earp was a fast talker; if Paine waited too long, he knew he'd be under arrest no matter what happened to the others.

It was up to him alone now.

He stopped to catch his breath and get his bearings. He'd outflanked his quarry already; two dozen yards more and he could double back and come up behind them, catching them just where he wanted them. He'd let them get away on the mountain, but he wouldn't make that mistake twice.

It was too bad, of course, that two men who'd helped bring law and order to the West would have to die in the crossfire along with one very important politician, but unfortunate accidents do happen.

He smiled to himself and started running again. He was about to be free of the terrible burden of his conspiracy. Then let Wyatt Earp tell any tale he wanted.

"There they are!" Hill hissed, pointing toward the police running from the ore pile into the millyard clutter on either flank. "They're making their move!" He fired twice, too quickly to inflict any damage. Comstock crouched beside him and took one carefully aimed shot, but it, too, fell short. He opened his gun to check the load.

Another salvo broke in on them, the bullets whizzing by like angry hornets. Hill dodged away, but too late; a slug ricocheted off a chunk of iron and caught him in the chest, spinning him around. He slid into a sitting position, a startled look on his face.

Comstock looked him over. "It's bad," he said as Hill, dazed, tried to lift his gun. His hand flopped away crazily as if he had no control over it.

Dahlman saw it and cackled. "You'll all be dead before this day's out."

Alvarez swung around on him and pointed the Smith and Wesson straight at Dahlman's heart. He started to thumb the hammer, but something made him think the better of it.

A thin grimace pulled at the big man's lips. "Law-abiding to the end, aren't you?" He laughed again. "It's a weakness, marshal. It's why men like you never amounted to shit." He coughed, choked, licked his lips. "It's why—"

Alvarez caught the faint sound, the scuffling of human feet on cinders. He looked hard at Dahlman, who'd heard it, too: the faintest flicker of anxiety and fear and relief all rolled together showed in his eyes. The grimace widened into defiance.

In a heartbeat, Alvarez knew.

Instinctively, he crouched down and swung around to face the threat.

The boom of Paine's Colt came from very near at hand. Then Ted Paine was on them, charging in at full speed.

Alvarez swung his gun into action, but he was too slow. The Colt boomed again. He sucked in his breath, knowing it would be his last. Somehow, Alvarez did not die.

Another gun fired from just behind Alvarez's head, and he saw Paine jerk sideways as if he'd run into an invisible wall. The gun behind Alvarez fired a second time. Paine took two steps backward and fired his Colt again, but his hand had already gone slack; when the hammer dropped, the recoil knocked the gun loose. Paine turned his head toward Alvarez and opened his mouth. It was filled with blood. One shot had smashed through his lungs and passed out his back, and the other had torn through his abdomen.

Ben Comstock squeezed the trigger one more time, and the hammer snapped down on a spent shell, but it didn't make any difference; Paine slid to his knees, then toppled over onto his side.

Alavarez knelt and picked up the Colt. "You bastard," he said.

"Never meant..." Paine whispered. He swallowed blood. "Never meant to hurt you." Then he twitched once and was still, his eyes already glazing over.

"Good riddance, I'd say," Comstock said matter-of-factly as he reloaded.

Alvarez gazed down at Paine and turned away, disgusted. "Thanks, Ben," he said.

"Don't mention it." He pushed the last shell into the cylinder and clicked it shut and nodded toward the others. "You better look to them."

Dahlman was unconscious on the ground. One of Paine's shots had hit him in the chest, and it was hard to tell whether the wound was mortal. There was no doubt about Hill: another bullet had struck him in the throat just below the Adam's apple, tearing out a jagged piece of flesh. He was sitting on the sooty earth with his legs stretched out in front of him and his hands in his lap as if he were a child. He coughed weakly, spraying a bloody mist into the air from the chest wound and lacerated windpipe.

Comstock scooped up Hill's little revolver and slipped it into his pocket.

"He'll be dead soon," Comstock said. "Too bad. We could use another shooter."

Someone some distance away barked out an order, and the shooting started again from a half-dozen well-hidden places.

"We might all be dead soon," Alvarez muttered.

"Earp must've let us down!" Comstock said.

Alvarez checked the flank, expecting to see the onslaught at any moment. "Seems so," he said.

"Well, let's give 'em what for!" Comstock fired his own revolver, then Hill's nickel-plated gun, until both needed reloading. The little weapon was so hot it jammed, and he threw it away in disgust.

"Let's get out of here," Alvarez said.

Comstock laughed at him. "Never ran from a fight and never will."

"Think about it," Alvarez said. He pointed toward the row of furnaces to the southeast. "If we go that way, maybe we can outrun 'em."

"Two old men?"

"They'll stop here to look after their dead. Besides, it ain't our fight. Not any longer." He pointed to the dead. "We got what we came for."

A bullet hit the piece of scrap iron less than a foot from Comstock's head with a loud *thunk*. He dodged away, and another cut through the air where his head had been with a high whine.

"Think about it," Alvarez repeated.

Comstock didn't need to think. "Then again, maybe this ain't our fight," he said, and he scrambled back to where Alvarez was hunkered down. "Just one thing, though. Where do we go if we get out of here? They'll be looking for us everywhere."

"I don't know. First things first," Alvarez said. Another salvo sent them sprawling. The police were getting closer. "It won't matter a damn if we don't get out of here soon."

"Sounds good to me."

Then they were up and moving, loping through the clutter of the millyard, pushing themselves until their lungs burned and their legs ached, moving away from Ulysses Hill and Ted Paine and the man who wanted to be governor, no matter what the cost.

They never saw Wyatt Earp, still arguing every step of the way, keeping himself between them and the Pueblo police, assuring his old friends of the few precious moments they needed to get away.

Chapter 25

ALVAREZ WAITED ON THE CUT BANK for Comstock to catch up. His leg was stiffening in the cold of dawn; it was going to be another very long day in a string of long days. Only the gray gelding beneath him seemed unconcerned. It browsed on the tough brown grama and ignored the quickening wind that pulled at its mane and tail.

Comstock's chestnut mare pulled up the bank. She was lathered, and Comstock was puffing.

Alvarez grinned in spite of the ache in his old wound. "I told you this horse had heart, dammit! I think it can outrun anything on four legs!" But even as he said it, he scanned the rolling plainsland for some sign that they were being followed. He saw nothing: so far, Earp and Masterson seemed as good as their word that they'd buy them the time they needed.

Comstock gulped for air, and the chestnut's nostrils flared at the smell of the gray, but it no longer pranced with the pent-up energy that Comstock had so admired when Cody had brought the horses around to their hiding place.

"Can't understand it," Ben wheezed. "That gray's carrying thirty more pounds than my mare."

"I'm just naturally light in the saddle," Alvarez said easily.

Comstock shook his head. "I reckon so. You'd think I would've noticed before now."

"You'd think."

The two men faced each other for a full minute across the ten feet that separated them. Not much more needed saying. After a time, Comstock stood in the stirrups and looked over his shoulder.

"I don't see anyone following," Alvarez said.

"That's good," Comstock said. "I had my doubts."

Alvarez knew what he meant. Lord knows, he'd had his own. After their escape from the mill, they'd hid out through the long afternoon and into the evening in the woods behind Gertrude Toothacker's place, waiting for the police to appear. There'd been great confusion for a while, but somehow they'd gone undetected until Gertrude spotted them in their hiding place. Once she'd finished getting her husband into the ground, she'd brought all the pallbearers back to her house for a big supper, and she'd known right where to look for the two fugitives. All in all, Alvarez figured he'd rather face the Pueblo police again than Gertrude. She'd given them a tongue-lashing that was no less painful because it was so well deserved. They'd made a travesty of her husband's funeral, she'd railed. They were scoundrels and rogues not fit to live with decent folks, and they ought to be ashamed of themselves. But when she'd finished, she'd promised them she'd steer the law away from the woods, and after dark, she'd even brought them some supper.

In the meantime, Wyatt Earp and Bat Masterson had busily spread the word that the politician found between the dying hunchback and the dead Denver police commissioner was mixed up in some nasty business of his own. Earp and Masterson traded shamelessly on their old notoriety in the process, but it also assured the whole story would get in the papers.

Which meant, in the peculiar way this new modern world worked, that Comstock's and Alvarez's good names would be cleared in due time. Eventually, they'd even be able to return to Colorado if they wanted.

But not just yet.

Ben Comstock shook his head and the freshening wind ruffled his hair. He was gaunt and feverish, the high energy of the previous day burned away like tinder in a forest fire, but he seemed to know what was on Alvarez's mind. "I don't know as I cotton to the idea of trusting my fate to Wyatt Earp and Bat Masterson." He made a face as if he had a bad taste in his mouth.

Alvarez grinned. "Don't have too much choice, do you?"

Comstock shook his head. "I reckon not." Then he stood in the saddle again and turned one last time toward Pueblo and the mountains beyond. "This is where I leave you, pard. I'm heading south from here."

"You sure you're strong enough to make it?"

"Fit as a fiddle. I always did heal quick." He told the lie with a sheepish grin. "'Sides, I can catch a train once I get to Raton. That ain't far."

"Far enough," Alvarez said, but he didn't get an answer. "Then I suppose I'm bound east." He thought of his wife waiting patiently for him, surely wondering what had become of him. And he thought of the inviting armchair with the white starched doilies where she'd want him to spend as much of the winter as he could stand. Maybe she'd never let him out of her sight again.

He knew he should be looking forward to the peace and quiet of that armchair in their tiny parlor.

Should be, but wasn't.

"It's a long way to Wichita," he added.

"Damn lonely country for an old man on horseback," Comstock said.

"Not as lonely as it used to be," Alvarez offered. He couldn't keep the note of regret out of his voice.

Comstock settled himself into the saddle. "Dammit, Thomas, I haven't had this much fun in fifteen years!"

Alvarez laughed and wiped a gloved hand across his eyes. The wind made them water. Or was it something more? Grief for something he'd lost for a long time, then found again, and now stood to lose for good? He shook his head. Damn foolishness to be thinking that way. "It's true," he said simply.

Comstock sniffed. "Well, take care, you old fool. Don't let some kid bushwhack you."

Alvarez took off his battered old black hat and waved it grandly, as Bill Cody might have. "You take care, too, Ben Comstock!"

Then he raked the gray with his heels and headed down the cut bank, across the nameless stream, and up the far side. He put the gelding into a steady walk toward the flat brown eastern horizon and didn't look back for a mile or so. When he did, Comstock and the chestnut were gone.

THE END

236